LESSONS FROM THE DEPRAVED

KINSLEY KINCAID

eBook ISBN: 978-1-7389892-0-1
Paperback ISBN: 978-1-7380934-5-8
Editing by Book Witch Author Services
Proofread by In The Shadows Author Services
Formatting by Charly Jade @ DesignsByCharlyy

DISCLAIMER

Please be aware this book contains many dark themes and subjects that may be uncomfortable/unsuitable for some readers. This book contains heavy themes throughout. Please keep this in mind when entering Lessons from the Depraved. Content warnings are listed on authors' social pages & website.

This book and its contents are entirely a work of fiction. Any resemblance or similarities to names, characters, organizations, places, events, incidents, or real people are entirely coincidental or used fictitiously.

If you find any genuine errors, please reach out to the author directly to correct it. Thank you.

Please do not distribute this material. It is a criminal offence!

This book is intended for 18+ only.

DEDICATION

This one is for me.
To making dreams a reality.
I'm proud of you.

PLAYLIST

messy is heaven - venbee, goddard.
Hate. - ThxSoMch
in bed with a psycho - Layto
Whore - Get Scared
Cyanide - Allistair
Love Language - Bizzy Crook
What do you want from me? - Bad Omens
Chemical - Post Malone
Under The Influence - Chris Brown
E-GIRLS ARE RUINING MY LIFE! - CORPSE,
Savage Ga$p
I Miss the Misery - Halestorm
Dangerous(feat. blackbear) - DeathbyRomy, blackbear
Ruin My Life - Zara Larson
Popular Monster - Falling In Reverse
CODE MISTAKE - CORPSE, Bring Me The Horizon
Loser - Sueco
Bad Things(with Camila Cabello) - Machine Gun Kelly
Or Nah - The Weekend, Ty Dolla $ign, Wiz Khalifa, DJ
Mustard
EAT SPIT! - Slush Puppy, Royal & the Serpent

Created by Twisted Kait and Kins
Spotify Playlist

SPECIAL NOTE FROM KINS

Meine deutschen Königinnen!

Ich sehe euch und ich bin besessen davon. Danke für all die Liebe und Unterstützung, die ihr mir geschenkt habt. Ich weiß, dass es für euch möglicherweise ein bisschen schwieriger ist, meine Bücher zu lesen, da sie nur auf englisch publiziert werden. Ich danke euch dafür, dass ihr euch trotzdem die Zeit nehmt, sie zu lesen. Es bedeutet mir alles! Ich schätze jeden einzelnen von euch so sehr! Ich bin über alle Maßen dankbar dafür!

xx kins

thank you tobifun for helping me translate!

My German, Queens!

I see you. And I'm obsessed. Thank you for all the love and support you have shown me. I know with my books being in English, it may take you longer to get through. Thank you for taking the time to read them regardless. It means the absolute world to me. I appreciate every single one of you so much! I'm forever grateful.

xx kins

CHAPTER 1

HUDSON

Music is pounding. The bass from the speakers causes the floor to shake beneath our feet. Lines of crushed Venom from the Noxious Boys decorate the cheap wooden coffee table along with bottles of beer and a bowl of pre-rolled joints. A group of us are off in another room, away from the main area of the party. Some guys have half-naked, desperate puck bunnies on their laps. Girls hoping that a hockey player will fuck them and fall in love.

It never happens. You can spot a puck bunny a mile away, and they are good for one thing: a quick fuck and chuck. I don't touch them with my cock. I don't need a chick thinking I want them or need them.

My teammate, Raiden, a Noxious Boy, sits across from me with a beer in his hand.

Thanks to him, we get a discount on our bulk purchases of Venom. Which helps on winning nights, because we go fucking big.

Our hockey team, the Jackals, have just won four in a row. We are on top of the motherfucking world and untouchable.

The more we win, the more attention we bring to Groveton, and the more money gets donated to our program and school. Which means this place lets us get away with anything and everything. If we killed someone tomorrow, they would cover it up as long as we kept winning.

Hockey in Texas is bigger than you think. Popularity of the sport here has risen, thanks to the pro teams. As a result, programs all over the state have gotten bigger and better. We aren't the favorite sport by any means, football will always hold that spot. But we can hold our fucking own.

We are at a players' frat house. We would never hold something like this at our off-campus place. My twin brother Landon and I don't need randoms going through our shit. We don't even bring cock hungry bitches back there. The odd close friend, sure. But fuck everyone else! We will get messed up and fill the frat houses with illegal drugs and underage drinking.

My brother and I are twenty-one. Seniors. But freshman meat shows up to these things. Barely eighteen and trying to fit in.

Speaking of, one has just poked her head in the room, "Hey, fuck off." I shout at the nosey bitch. "You're rude," she hisses back at me.

"Yeah, and you're a nosey cunt. Go."

She just stands there looking at me. I'm not sure what the fuck she is waiting for?

There's a hot brunette sitting next to me, I think her name is Katie or something. She's here for the drugs. At every party I have seen her at, she is always where the drugs are.

Katie takes a hit off her joint and must feel my eyes on her. Opening my mouth, she blows the smoke from her mouth to mine. Smoke fills my lungs on my deep inhale, adding to the high from the venom I had earlier. Exhaling it, and still looking at her, I whisper, "Suck."

Biting her lip, Katie looks down at my cock then back over my shoulder where I assume the nosey bitch is still lurking, hopefully. It's the only reason I'm doing this. Passing the joint to whoever is next to her, Katie slides off the couch to her knees, and I spread my legs wide, undoing the buttons of my pants, and sliding the zipper down. I can feel the eyes of the room on us when Katie's petite hands grasp my waistband, pulling my pants and boxers down to my knees all at once. My cock is hard, precum leaking from the tip. She grabs her hair, which is hanging loose and bunches it together and throws it over her shoulder before putting my cock in her mouth. My eyes focus on her plump lips working my shaft. Taking me deep, she doesn't gag. The girl is a champ. Katie's tongue strokes the underside of my shaft as I continue to ram into the back of her throat. She looks up, through her eyelashes, drool trickling down her chin as her eyes water.

"You see this? This is how you suck cock, you nosey bitch." I say to the room, knowing that she is still in the doorway. Probably getting off on this.

Katie pauses at my words. The fuck is she doing?

"Keep sucking. Slurp on my cock," I demand, grabbing hold of her hair at the crown of her head.

My hips buck, and now she starts to gag. Fucking right. I continue my assault on her throat, feeling my orgasm building.

"Fucking take it." I rasp through heavy breaths.

My legs tingle. I'm not showing this girl any mercy.

Ropes of my warm cum begin coating her throat. "Take it. Swallow it all."

I don't let up as I continue to fuck her face, working through my orgasm as my cum continues to shoot out of my cock into her mouth. Her eyes are tearing, streaming down her face. It's fucking perfection.

As my orgasm begins to die down, I let go of her hair and throw my head back onto the couch. Turning slightly, I smile at Ms. Nosey. Catching her biting her lip, she looks mortified at being caught enjoying it.

We hold each other's gaze for a moment; she seems frozen in place, before she scurries out of the room.

"Ok, Katie. I'm good. Off my cock now."

Her mouth slides off my shaft, and she uses her tongue to lick my tip clean before she leans back on her heels and stands up, moving back to her spot on the couch, and wiping her mouth. I bring my pants back up and over my hips, tucking my semi hard cock back in and doing up my pants.

I look over at Landon. He is smiling and shaking his head at me, then sits forward, dollar bill rolled and placed up to his nose, snorting a line of venom. He returns my stare as he wipes his nose, "You're such a dick."

Like this is earth shattering information. This is something I have been well aware of since birth, thanks to our father.

Landon was the saint, and I'm the spawn of Satan. Which makes sense if you think about it. My father is Satan. But that is a story for another day, or never at all.

Giving my brother the finger, he laughs at me. The effects of the venom and weed are taking over. Best fucking high. The venom is a hallucinogenic and elevates you. I feel like I'm floating. Landon has colors radiating off him. Vibrant pinks and blues that if I were to touch them, they would ripple through the air.

I'm sure my eyes are hooded. Laughter leaves my mouth, and it echoes in the room. That's the effects from the weed mixed in.

My mind wanders, knowing we are so close to the end. I can taste it on my tongue. Bursts of sweet grapes erupting. Fizzy bubbles popping. There is one more game before Christmas break starts. The last Christmas break of our college career. Cannot fucking wait to get out of here. One more semester, then the world is ours. We are free to do whatever the fuck we want.

I have a couple more exams that I don't give a fuck about, but will magically pass thanks to our Athletics Student Advisor—if she knows what's good for her.

Banks Lewis. She's new. Maybe late twenties, early thirties. From what we have found out, this is her first big gig out of college. She is snatched as fuck, too. It's a nice change from our previous advisor who had retired. We gave her gifts, flirted, and envelopes of cash magically appeared in her home mailbox and our grades would appear as passing. We have to maintain a C minus average to stay on the team.

But fuck thinking about school right now. We just won four in a row. The guys and I are on top of the fucking world and this high is too fucking good to not enjoy.

CHAPTER 2

BANKS

The air is crisp.

December in Groveton, Texas can be chilly. The leaves on the trees have fallen, and the lush green grass is more of a dull brown this time of year. A cool winter breeze blows, causing goosebumps to decorate my skin as I stand outside of my white Honda Civic. The sky is gray, filled with clouds floating low to the ground. They do this each winter. The sun tries to peek through, sometimes the clouds allow it. Most times, they don't.

The campus is buzzing from the weekend. Our hockey team has won their fourth game in a row. Being the team's Athletics Student Advisor, I was at the game. The guys are playing like each pass and every goal is effortless. I watch their practices, where they spend hours going over plays and practicing faceoffs. The more time they spend together, the stronger their chemistry becomes. Which shows on the ice.

Watching them is like watching poetry on ice.

Thanks to my dad, I've always been a fan of hockey and it was a dream to get this job this past summer. Now that my first semester is nearing its end, I have no regrets.

This is my passion.

This team. This job. This campus. These students.

I walk through the parking lot to the paved pathway lined with benches, shrubs and bare trees on my daily walk to my office. Old brick buildings are scattered around it. Students are bundled up with book bags on their backs racing to their morning classes. The arena is located on the edge of campus, the rink is a decent size for a college. It can seat up to five thousand people, the outside walls are white and gray with the green Jackal logo decorating each side. On top of the entrance doors is a giant sign that lights up at night with *Barlowe Arena*. I take it all in as I approach. As I do everyday, wondering how I got so lucky.

My life hasn't been roses.

Don't get me wrong, my childhood was amazing, but these past few years have been hell. And now, I'm all alone.

Getting this job was the first bit of light I have seen in a while.

That doesn't matter now. Shaking my head to rid me of the memories that creep up every so often, especially around this time of year. Christmas.

I let out a deep breath when I arrive at the arena doors. Grabbing my card from my black winter puffer jacket, I pass it over the scanner, and it turns green, unlocking the door for me. As soon as I enter, I walk past the concessions and store that sells the team's merchandise. Just past the is a sign that says staff only, and I scan my pass over it, unlocking the heavy steel door, painted in black. Twisting the silver handle, I have to use all my strength to push it open. Surely I have to be building muscle from doing this everyday. The quietness of the hallway is no more. As soon as I enter the area, loud grunts bounce off the walls, the clicking of weight machines echo and deep male voices fill my ears. All of this brings a smile to my face. Breathing in through my nose, the distinct smells of sweat and testosterone invade my senses with a hint of ice rink. If you have been to a hockey arena, you know this smell. No amount of fans airing the place out or odor spray can get rid of it. I think it's a part that those of us who are in this world would actually miss if it disappeared.

But this here, it's my home.

"Yo, Ms. Lewis. Looking good as always," Trace Barlowe, our goalie, shouts at me then whistles, causing me to laugh on my way past the weight room and wave in response. I'm one of the only females who support the team besides a few PT's who are also students here. The catcalls are fine, they don't bother me. It's harmless banter, in my opinion.

A few other guys laugh at his comment.

"Good for you, Trace," I yell back as I head to my office.

I grab hold of the keyring that holds my office key and unlock my door. The room is pretty bare, with only a dark wooden desk, a couple of chairs on one side, with my desk chair on the other, along with a phone, and a few locked filing cabinets. I don't have a desktop computer. I prefer a laptop. This way, if we are at an away game, I can still work and correspond with their professors, as needed. My job is to stay on top of the guys when it comes to their grades and homework. For many of them, hockey is a passion and they are here on a scholarship. The NHL isn't in their future. I make sure they are successful academically in order to remain on the team, keep their scholarship, and have a degree when they walk out of here. I know the odd one may make it to the big leagues. They may not think education is important, but once they hit thirty-five and are forced to retire, they will regret not taking it seriously. So, I'm the one to push them now to get the degree, then they don't live with regret later. Sure, if they make a fuck load of cash, they can live off it. But to go from a fast-paced lifestyle to nothing isn't in their DNA; none of these kids have ever had to sit still longer than summer break. Even then, there are hockey camps and leagues many jump into.

As inappropriate as it sounds, I ride these guys. Constantly emailing or texting, making sure their assignments have been handed in, their tests are studied for, and if their grades are slipping, I arrange tutors. These kids will not fail under my watch, but it is up to them to work for it. I can only give them the tools, the rest is up to them. Sometimes, I bring Coach Taylor in. He can kick their asses into shape like no other. Fortunately, most of the time they are good kids and listen to me.

Setting my backpack down behind my desk, I take a seat in my chair and grab my laptop out of my bag and I open it up to turn it on. Within seconds of entering my password, I have two email notifications.

The guys are mid way through exam week. These emails can only mean one thing.

Someone has fucked up.

CHAPTER 3

LANDON

My phone dings on my nightstand.
Who the fuck is bothering me this early in the morning?!

My eyes remain closed as I roll over in my bed, wearing just my boxers with my inked chest exposed.

Reaching my hand out, I begin feeling around until I find it. Clicking the side button, I open my eyes to see it's only 8am.

Fuck my life.

Then I see a text from Coach.

Shit. This can't be good.

Today was an optional workout day. So I know I'm not in trouble for that. Closing my eyes and raking my fingers through my black wavy hair, I try and think. What did I do?

The guy has eyes everywhere. It could be anything. I'm in one of my anti-social moods, so I haven't gone out much other than to write my exams.

Fuck, come on. Think.

Yeah, when it comes to Coach. I'm a pussy. The guy doesn't send a text to be polite. He only sends texts or calls if you're in a giant pile of shit.

What the fuck did I do? Before I can figure it out, my brother, Hudson, comes storming in.

"We are fucked."

Parking in the rink lot, I get out of my black Range Rover, and close the door behind me with Hudson following. Hud drove in with me after barging in my room and informing me that the text was a group chat for just us. And that Coach wanted us in his office within the next twenty minutes or he would come to us.

No way we were letting him come to the house. This is our sanctuary.

Hud and I got dressed as fast as we could and rushed to the rink.

We both had no fucking clue what we did. We also had no idea our coach knew how to group text, which was massively impressive. But it also means he is insanely pissed. Face red, horns showing kind of pissed.

It would make sense for Hudson to be getting in shit for something. He is loud about most things he does. Me though, I'm the quiet twin. The unsuspecting twin. I can get away with loads more than he can. But I haven't done shit this week. So the fact that we were both called in, has me confused as fuck.

Hud has his pass out, ready to go as we approach the front doors to let us in. Racing through them, we jog toward the locker room. Passing the staff entrance, our footsteps can be heard echoing in the quiet cement hallways, painted white and gray with the green Groveton Jackal logo.

"Hurry the fuck up," Hud shouts as I trail behind him.

Rolling my eyes, I give him the finger. I'm right fucking behind him.

"I fucking saw that."

No, you didn't.

We reach the green double doors at the end of the long hallway, and Hudson swipes his badge, pushing on the door to let us in.

The doors open up directly to the hallway that leads to the locker room, weight room, PT area and staff offices. The heavy steel doors close behind us, and make a loud click when they fall back into place.

"Get the fuck in my office. NOW!" Hud looks back at me, wide-eyed, as I throw my head back.

Laughter from the guys who showed up for an optional workout follows Coach's shouting. Wasting no time, we start the walk of shame. Both of us are in black sweats, Jordans on our feet and our team's dark green hoodies. My hood hangs over my head while Hudson lets his dark hair show, shorter on the sides and longer in the front.

We both take one more deep breath as we approach the office. The door is open and my heart races in anticipation.

Rounding the doorway, my eyes meet Coach's. He is sitting behind his desk, leaning back in his chair with his hands behind his head. He's wearing his usual dark green team tracksuit, the wind jacket is unzipped showing his white team shirt underneath.

It's who I see next that makes all of this click.

Ms. Lewis.

She is sitting on the brown couch against his wall. Her hair is long, black, and wavy hanging over her shoulders. Petite with a great ass. That is something I have come to notice throughout her first semester with the team. Her green eyes look back at me, freckles run across the bridge of her button nose. She is nervous. Biting her bottom lip gives it away. Her right leg is trembling with anticipation. We keep it pretty casual around here. Ms. Lewis, Banks, is in black skinny jeans, black high-top converse and an oversized cream knitted sweater. She's started to pick at her cuticles, and as I look up again, I catch her looking back at me.

I wink at her, letting her know I've caught her and her eyes immediately shift to Coach.

"Sit the fuck down," he barks at us. Regaining my attention.

My brother and I both take a seat in the chairs in front of his desk. Looking over to Hudson, he turns his head briefly to look at me. His eyes cut to the side, silently telling me to look back over where I was just looking.

That's when I realized it.

Why we are here.

We have a fucking narc in our midst, boys.

CHAPTER 4

BANKS

I guess I forgot to mention the fifteen grand I found under my apartment door earlier this week. That's not why the Cooper's have been called into Coach's office, though.

I have no idea where the money came from. It was divided into separate envelopes, a grand in ten smaller envelopes, then five grand in another labeled *'yours'*. When I get nervous, which I am now, things that aren't even relevant enter my head and I feel like just spitting it out.

There is no reason for me to feel this way.

Well, maybe a tiny bit of a reason. The Coopers are like gods around here. Hudson, our power house captain, and first line center is destined to play pro and is wildly outspoken. Landon is quieter with a friendlier and softer face, but also intimidating. You never know what he is thinking. But with his piercing blue eyes, he is always watching, always observing. I watch people, and he is a curious man. Landon plays defense for us. Both boys are seniors, built with those hockey thighs and asses, tall and attractive.

A girl can look.

After I've just been side eye'd by Landon, they may just look more terrifying than attractive. Plus, I'm the reason they've been called in.

The early morning emails came from their professors. If you are on the team, you need to maintain a C minus average. Coach Taylor holds them to a higher standard. B minus, otherwise you are on probation. Have to attend all optional days and bag skates on weekends, game or no game. You skate.

Landon passed his arts exams, his major, but barely passed his Statistics class. It brought his average below what the coach finds acceptable.

Hudson, on the other hand, was alarming.

He is a business major, he failed most of his exams, but somehow still passed his courses. Like his brother, his average is well below the B minus coach expects.

It's my job to bring all grades to Coach. He likes being involved in their education and holding them accountable like adults and not kids. When I got the email from their professors with their grades, with still an exam each to go, I couldn't ignore it. Even if they both pass their last one with flying colors, it won't bring their average up high enough.

I can feel eyes on me. Burning into my skin.

"Look at me, not her." Coach barks at the twins.

My focus is on Coach. Not the boys now. This is also my first serious meeting with guys from the team and coach. Normally it's check in's, helping the students out and setting up resources for them to take advantage of.

I'm sure this is the first of many uncomfortable meetings in my foreseeable future once they are put on probation.

Coach rotates his laptop around, showing both of them their grades.

"What the fuck is this? You two have never been an issue with grades in the past. But you have decided to fuck off in the brain cell department in your senior year? Hudson, you have failed every final so far. I would bet my left nut the exam tomorrow will have the same result. Yet magically you're still passing the class. I don't know whose dick you sucked for this, but it's worked—barely!" Coach shakes his head still in disbelief, then continues onto Landon.

"Landon. Son, I'm disappointed. Never did I think you would be sitting here in this situation. I know, *we* know, you can do better. Both of you are below the B minus average I expect all my players to have. A document I have all you sign at the beginning of the year. I want you to fucking succeed out in this forsaken world once you leave Groveton. Bag skates on weekends, game or no game. All workouts are mandatory. Midterms next semester determine if you stay on probation for the rest of the season or not. Thank you for fucking up my weekends for the next couple months. Now get the fuck out of my sight." Coach barks while closing his laptop screen. Both boys stand up, faces neutral, but their chests are heaving.

"We start the first weekend of the next semester, 7am," Coach adds before the twins leave. I stay seated in place.

Landon's head turns slightly toward me one more time

31

as he and Hudson walk toward the door. Before leaving, both respond to the coach's instruction, "Yes, Coach." They leave the room, closing the door behind them.

A deep exhale leaves my lungs, my hands slightly tremble.

"Banks. If those boys do anything to take this out on you, you tell me. They earned their probation by not fulfilling my expectations of them. Hudson is the goddamn captain, he should know better. He should set an example to the others. Landon lets his brother influence him. The guy is a good kid, but unfortunately, he is in this with Hudson now. We don't have any games or practices over Christmas break. Take this time to relax and refresh because we are chasing the finals come January, and the team will need you more than ever for support." I nod in response. Coach has always been good to me. Helping me find my footing in this new role and supporting me and my decisions with the guys.

"Thank you, Coach, I appreciate that." I half smile while standing up and start walking toward his office door.

"You did good. Don't let this weigh too heavily on your shoulders, Banks. Helping me hold them accountable in their academics is why you are here. Remember that."

Before closing the door behind me, I turn around "Thanks again, Coach, that means a lot."

I walk back to my office, a couple doors down, half dazed, and my shoulder bumps into someone immediately jolting me.

Looking at his chest, I hold my own, and begin apologizing profusely, "I am so sorry. I didn't see you. I wasn't paying attention." As my eyes move up the strong torso covered in the signature green team hoodie. Continuing up past the strong jawline with some dark stubble, the piercing blue eyes cause my own to widen. His hood is still hanging over his head. Landon.

He chuckles at me when he notices me realizing it is him who I just ran into.

Shit.

"Ms. Lewis. I'm sure you are very sorry. But I'm not." Then he smirks at me.

I blink at him, unable to move my lips to respond. My heart is racing and could burst out of my chest at any moment.

I am not normally intimidated this easily. These boys, there's something about them that terrifies me. I had a job to do, and I did it. They will need to get over it. By midterms, this will be done and forgotten.

Nodding at his comment, I move to walk around him, not wanting to engage further and cause an unnecessary scene.

Keeping my pace the same, to show I'm not bothered, I walk to my office and close the door softly behind me.

Just one more day until Christmas break.

CHAPTER 5

LANDON

She fucked me.
She fucked my brother.
I might be quiet, but do not fucking cross us because it's the quiet ones you should worry about.

"Didn't you give her the cash?" Hudson barks from next to me while we drive back home. Slamming my hand against the wheel, "Of course I fucking did. Fifteen grand. I even divided it up for her so she wouldn't have to. All she had to do was give them to our professors, like every other year, and keep five for herself to keep her fucking mouth shut."

"Do you think the old bat that retired didn't fill her in on our arrangement?" Hud questions. Throwing my head back on the seat in frustration, "I mean, it's fucking possible. Why the fuck wouldn't she, though? It was a major fucking part of her job."

"I won't be quiet about this. I am fucking pissed, bro" an evil laugh leaves my brother's mouth. The guy is always loud, so his declaration is nothing but on brand. Pulling up our driveway, we live off campus in a large, old, red brick two-story house. It has a white front porch, detached garage, complete with the white picket fence to match. We have large trees in the front to provide extra privacy, which we require. Since leaving home, privacy has become something that we highly value. At home, dad didn't give us any privacy. Cameras were everywhere, including our rooms. He was always watching us, always itching to punish us, if given the chance. When people say Hud is the spawn of Satan, he doesn't dispute it, because we both are. Our old man is Satan, and it was the best day ever when we got the news that we got into Groveton, hundreds of miles away from our personal prison. Hockey was a release, our outlet while at home. Along with art, for me. I love drawing, and have dabbled in tattooing because of it. Something to keep me busy when school is done and Hud is off being a pro somewhere. Hearing the car door slam jolts me out of thoughts. Hud is already racing up the porch stairs. Turning off the Rover, I get out and follow behind him.

We are greeted by dark wood floors and staircase with a wrought-iron banister when we walk inside. Hud looks back at me, "I'll be in the basement. I have an idea." Then rushes off toward the kitchen to the basement door.

The fuck? He never goes into the basement. It's unfinished and cold as fuck.

Whatever, I'm sure he will show me once he's done. Until then, I'm going back to bed. Hud has one more exam, and I'm home free until next semester starts. May as well bask in my freedom while I have it.

I rush up the stairs and down the hall to my room. I won the master suite after an intense game of rock, paper, scissors.

Fair is fair.

Kicking off my shoes and pulling my hoodie off, I drop it onto the black carpet, and fall onto the black silk sheets and comforter that cover my bed. My desk off to the side is full of my sketchbooks and art supplies with a stained-glass lamp, lined up against the dark gray wall.

Why does she have to be hot and seem so innocent? Not that the hot part will deter us, but her fucking innocence may.

Who am I kidding? It won't. It will take less to break her into a million tiny pieces. She'll be lucky if she ends up in a psych ward after we are through with her. Those green eyes, full of tears, will be beautiful. Streaming down her porcelain skin. I hope she begs for us to stop. To leave her alone. I hope she promises to run and never come back while on her knees before us, pleading. Such a pathetic display.

My skin gets goosebumps at the thought of it all. These types of thoughts aren't new. Relishing in someone else's demise. I often think about the things I would do to my father. I'd make it slow and painful. To suffer like the rest of us did. Lingering resentment keeps these thoughts fueled.

Before closing my eyes and falling back to sleep. A smile tries to spread across my face, but I fight it back.

Banks will get what she deserves, ruthless and unrelenting pain and regret.

HUDSON

This may have been the best fucking idea I have had... ever!

Bouncing on the balls of my shoes with excitement.

My sperm donor always said, 'If you can't beat them, join them.'

The spawn of Satan is becoming Satan, just for her.

I pull out my phone and dial my teammate and good friend, Raiden. He picks up after the second ring. "Yo, bro. I need some Venom."

"Yeah man, I'm out now. I'll drop some off, no problem." Then he hangs up. Raiden is not one for formalities. He's like my brother that way, maybe that's why they work so well and play defense together.

Banks Lewis, run little girl. You are now our prey.

CHAPTER 6

BANKS

Yesterday was the last day of school until next semester. Some of the team left a few gift cards on my desk for me, and Trace left me his number, which made me laugh before throwing it in the garbage.

My apartment is only a five-minute drive from campus and I sigh as I look out the window to find a blue sky with clusters of gray clouds, the perfect weather for Christmas. The only thing that would make it better would be my dad still being around. This will be my first Christmas without him and all alone. It's time to make new traditions, it's ok. I've got this.

But I have never felt so restless. Sitting still makes me

anxious, like I could crawl out of my own skin. A shiver encompasses my body and goosebumps erupt across my flesh. The first holiday alone must be provoking this unease. I just need to get through this one holiday and the rest will be a breeze.

I'm wearing our team hoodie, white with the green Jackal logo on the front with a pair of black leggings and Ugg boots. My long black hair is in a high, messy pony. I've added a bit of mascara to coat my lashes, while concealer hides the dark color under my eyes. This restless feeling has been causing some sleepless nights. Once this holiday is over, everything will be fine.

Pulling my phone out of my hoodie pocket to check the time, it's nearly 5 pm. Our final game before break is tonight, at home. We play our closest rival, Richardson College, tonight. The game is bound to be a good one, our guys are relentless against them. They push and push until Richardson finally snaps, forcing a penalty. It's great hockey.

Great hockey I'm going to be late for if I don't hurry.

With my mind occupied with something other than Christmas, I grab my car keys off my front entrance table and head out.

Traffic was lighter than normal tonight.

Campus is like a ghost town except for a small crowd gathering at Barlowe Arena. Locals and the diehard fans of either team are here. I park my car in my normal spot. The sun has gone down, the light posts begin turning

42

on, lighting the parking lot and illuminating the pathway through Groveton.

The evening chill pricks my skin once I've exited the car. I shove both hands into my hoodie pocket as I make my way toward the arena. A few others are on the same path, heading in the same direction. A small group of students are laughing at something one of them has said, from what I can faintly hear.

They don't have a care in the world, the worries and stress of adulting haven't set in for them yet. The real world can be scary and unpredictable, full of joy and pain. I hope they remember this moment in time when it feels like their world is ending. That it isn't all doom and gloom. The good times exist amongst the dark, you just need to remember them.

A slight breeze blows against me, and my ponytail brushing against my nape brings me back to the present. The bare trees sway and the dried, dead leaves on the ground rustle. I've walked through most of campus while lost in my thoughts. Still caught up in the dread from earlier, when I don't want to be. Being here at the game should help at least for a few hours.

The vibration of my phone startles me as I continue walking toward the arena. Pulling it out of my pocket, it's a message from Flynn, another staff member here at Groveton. He is a counselor for the students. My heart drops. What's wrong?

Coming to a stop. My heart is racing, he doesn't usually text. The advisors and counseling staff all have each other's numbers. Our students could have crossovers and we like to keep each other in the loop, as needed and within reason, without breaking any confidentiality. I swipe my screen and open the text.

Flynn: 11pm
Tonight
End of semester fire at the
abandoned Grange Manor

I read it at least five more times, my face scrunching up as I decipher his message. My first thought is thank goodness everyone is ok. My second thought is, do the staff actually do this? They must. Why else would he text this? Unless it's a last-minute thing, I would think I would have heard about it sooner if it was tradition. But, I guess it could be fun. Let loose for a few hours before going back to my lonely apartment. The Grange Manor is an amazing location, too. It's kind of creepy, something I love. Spooky season is a favorite of mine. And the best part is it's far away from students.

The Manor is well off campus, at least a thirty-minute drive. The family that once lived there are rumored to have just left one day and never returned. Absolutely no student would find us there. It could be fun to check it out after the game.

Replying to Flynn,

Sounds great! See you then.

When I start walking again, I see the arena has a slight line to get in, which is exciting. Games are so much more fun with more people in the stands. The players thrive off the energy of the crowd. I pull my lanyard out from under my hoodie where my staff badge hangs, and show it to the ticket kids at the doors, "Hey, Ms. Banks. Happy Holidays," one says to me. It's a volunteer position where a group of students rotate doing it, tonight it's Jaden and Kane. They are good kids.

Some volunteer because it will look good on their resume when applying for jobs after they graduate. Others, like Kane and Jaden, love the game and want to be involved in any way they can. Plus, they get free tickets to watch after the doors close.

"Happy holidays, guys!" I smile back at them as I pass through the doors.

The main concourse is packed with people. Some are in line for drinks and snacks, others just hanging out before puck drop. I love it all, nothing better than game night at home. Weaving through the crowd, I pass the staff entrance door off the main hallway and continue walking toward the double doors the players go through, they are closer to the dressing room. Scanning my badge, the doors unlock and I push one open and slip through, making sure it closes behind me.

These guys sometimes have a handful of females waiting at these doors. The last thing Coach needs is one sneaking in. He would lose his shit. The guy doesn't mess around when it comes to game night.

This is my home game routine: come to the arena; wish the guys luck; and then go to my regular seat, center ice behind the bench.

Just before walking into the dressing room, I put my hand over my eyes, slightly covering them like a visor, "Is everyone decent?" I shout into the room.

"Ms. Lewis, where would the fun in that be?" Trace hollers back at me. Cheeky bastard, I have to give him that much.

"Yeah, come on in Ms. Lewis," Brandon yells. The

guys call him Smiley because he is always happy, not the brightest bulb, but he doesn't let that get him down.

Removing my hand visor from my face, I walk in. Guys are lined on either side sitting on their bench at their wooden lockers. They have a shelf and hanger space behind them, which houses their gear and jersey. Coach Taylor walks in behind me, his one hand goes on my shoulder, making me aware he is there. I try to move out of the way as he begins to move his hand, it brushes faintly along my back, which is not normal for him but I'm sure he means no harm by it.

Bringing my attention back to the team, "I just wanted to wish you guys a great Christmas break and I hope you kick Richardson's ass!"

The guys cheer, "Fuck yeah, Ms. Lewis." Trace stands, and fist pumps into the air bringing a smile to my face.

My eyes wander over to the twins.

Landon's face remains expressionless as he looks at me. His eyes feel like they are looking through me and into my soul. It's eerie. Moving my gaze to Hudson, he is wrapping his stick with precision and focus with his dark hair hanging slightly over his forehead. His lips move slightly. Mumbling something only Landon hears. The only reason I know this is because Landon slightly nods in response.

"You got it, Banks." Hudson casually says while side-eyeing me and winking. A few of the guys whistle after it. I'm not bothered. I'm sure they are still pissed at me, for their grades and having to bag skates on weekends after break until midterms. It makes sense, I'm the problem, in their eyes.

"Well, on that note. I'm going to let you guys get to it," I say to no one in particular before turning around and heading out of the locker room.

Coaches' eyes linger on me more than is socially

acceptable while I turn to leave. Which is also completely out of character for him. Maybe he is having an off night... I hope.

I hear the guys do their team chant as I walk down the hall,

"Check Hard. Play Hard. Fuck Hard."

"Shut the fuck up, would ya?" Coach scolds them. He hates it. I think it's funny, but I would never admit that to them.

Five minutes left in the third period.

We are annihilating Richardson College. Our team has so much skill and raw talent. Our defense is on fire.

And you know what they say, *'Defense wins Championships.'*

Raiden King, who I hear the guys call Radar sometimes, when they aren't calling him King, can zero in on that puck and stop it from reaching our goalie 99% of the time. Either stopping it with his body or stick. Landon is paired with him, and he is just as aggressive as Raiden, but in his own silent assassin way. He can predict the move before it's made. Then he challenges the opposing player until they can't complete their play. Between the two of them, it's like watching a symphony on ice. It's cliche, I know, but let's call a spade a spade.

The sound of loud cheers breaks me from my thoughts.

Focusing on the ice, I see players from Richardson skate from their end to ours. A couple sticks lay abandoned, along with a few pairs of gloves. Hudson, our captain, is holding a few guys back from the other team. Trace

Barlowe, our goalie, has started to skate toward center ice. Fuck.

I stand to get a better view of what is happening on the ice. Raiden has one guy in a headlock, helmet off punching him repeatedly. Droplets of blood stain the ice, I'm sure it's from the guy he is pounding on. Meanwhile, I spot Smiley against the boards, being held there by another Richardson player. Landon has skated up behind him and has the guy by the collar of his jersey trying to pull him off. Then he knees him in the back of his leg, causing the player to drop. Smiley skates out of the way, helping the rest of his team keep the other team's players back, while Raiden continues to beat on the guy. Landon jumps on his guy, who is now laying on the ice. Landon punches at the guy's ribs while practically sitting on him. More cheering ignites the area, moving my attention back to Barlowe. Him and the Richardson goalie have just dropped gloves.

What in the fuck did I miss while I was zoned out?

Leaning over to the person next me I ask, "What the fuck happened? I completely missed it."

Buddy chuckles while keeping his eyes on the display in front of us, "Beaumont high-sticked Smiley, then checked him hard into the boards. That's who King has right now. And after that, all hell broke loose. No fucking idea why the goalies are fighting, but this is fucking amazing."

No one messes with Smiley and gets away with it. The guy is shockingly good at this game and a clean player. It's all adding up now.

The refs and linesmen are trying to separate them all but it's utter chaos on the ice, whistles blowing, discarded equipment everywhere, both teams' coaching staff have left the bench. Coach is trying to stop the goalie fight, which is tragic. Goalie fights are rare and amazing. Not that I condone violence, but it's hockey.

Finally, the refs are able to separate a few of the guys. Hudson is pushing some of the other team's players back to their designated bench area.

A voice comes over the loudspeaker.

"Ten minute major, unsportsmanlike conduct, Raider King. Ten minute major, unsportsmanlike conduct Landon Cooper. Five minute major, Mark Beaumont high-sticking." Damn.

Thankfully the goalies were left out of the penalties But our best D duo are out for the rest of the game now All three head back to their dressing rooms. No poin sitting in the box with only two minutes left in the game.

The ice team is out trying to scrape and level out where the bloodstains are. Guys are collecting the gloves and sticks scattered. Coach's face is red.

The guys skate off the ice, smiling. They aren't ashamed

We are up 4-2, I have faith our guys can keep the lead even while playing four on five for the rest of the game out it's not going to be fun.

As part of our power play team, Hudson takes cente ce for the faceoff. He wins it. We have control of the puck Now we just have to keep it.

The minutes pass. My heart races. We cannot let Richardson in our zone.

'*Last minute of play in the third period.*' Sounds over the loudspeaker.

We are all on our feet. Clapping and cheering. Come on boys.

I'm bouncing on the balls of my feet. They are killing this penalty perfectly.

The buzzer sounds.

The crowd gets even louder. A smile spreads across m

CHAPTER 7

HUDSON

What a way to close out the first half of the season. Shit.

And we fucking won. Of course we did. Never was that a doubt in my mind, even after the brawl and penalties. We are on a winning streak for a fucking reason. We are the best. The numbers and stats don't lie.

After the game, we showered and changed quickly. We needed to get to Grange Manor before she did.

Banks Lewis.

Bitch fucked with the wrong family. Plus, she kept the cash. Did she seriously think we would do nothing about it?

I am the captain of the team. I have a responsibility on

my shoulders that the others don't. According to Coach, I have to lead by example on and off the ice. After hours, what Coach doesn't know won't hurt him. If he only fucking knew.

And after tonight, Landon is even more on the shit list than I am. Along with Raiden. Even though it was kind of epic. Highlights are definitely going to make the rounds. Coach will be mortified, while the guys will be lapping up the attention. Then we will all get punished for it. I'm sure Raiden will be bag skated just as hard as we will be once we are all back from break. The guy has been itching for a fight. I've felt it on and off the ice. So when this one presented itself, he took it. So did Landon, the guy has some pent up frustration. It's usually a shock to people. Not me, though.

I'm his twin. We are weirdly connected. He is as fucked up as I am. Just not as loud about it. As the Spawn of Satan, I am very loud about most things I do. The more I know that what I'm doing would piss my father off, the louder I get, the better it feels and the more I don't give a fuck. Soulless. Heartless. Heathen. Are a few terms I have heard thrown my way.

I fucking love it.

And I don't fucking care.

"Bro. She's here." Landon whispers.

I rub the palms of my hands together, *it's go time baby.*

I've been working hard on this. Finally made use of our basement, too.

Landon got Flynn to text naughty Banks Lewis. Inviting her to an end-of-year-party. So naïve. She played into our plan perfectly. Just as predicted.

We cut the lock and drove right in. We aren't the first to break in, we won't be the last. They have to relock the gate monthly. Oddly enough, they have never installed cameras. But I won't question it. It's working to our advantage tonight. The old Grange Manor is made of large tan brick blocks, and is two stories tall. The peaked roof is black, along with the front door. The lights from her car beam across the abandoned property.

Once her headlights turn off, Landon and I unbuckle our seat belts. The click breaking the silence and anticipation. We are both wearing head to toe black. Landon disconnected his interior lights when we got here. She won't see us coming.

BANKS

It's pitch black out. No sign of anyone else being here. No cars. No fire. No people.

Pulling out my phone, I check the text. It says tonight. Looking at the time, it's nearly 11pm. Maybe I'm early? Like in high school or even college, if someone says the party starts at 9pm, they really mean midnight.

Slipping my phone back in my pocket, I decide to kill some time and explore this old place. I've heard stories about it. The family just left. Leaving this place locked up and never to return. It's bizarre.

I chuck my keychain lanyard onto my passenger seat, no one's around to steal my car anyway. I'm not worried. Getting out, the crisp winter air sends a chill over my body, I close the door and set off to explore.

Using my phone flashlight to light the way, I shine it in front of me as I walk from the driveway to the front door. Dead leaves and fallen branches crack beneath my feet. A large archway covers the front door, and my hand reaches out, making contact with the cold metal handle. I try turning it, but don't make much progress. It's locked.

The air smells of winter. Until it doesn't.

My nose picks up a faint smell of a musk. Before I can turn around, a deep voice whispers, "The party is just about to begin, Banks." Their warm breath on my ear causes me to freeze. Then, I feel a tiny sting on my neck. Raising my hand to it, I find nothing is there.

There's a whisper in my other ear, but it sounds like a mile away. "Enjoy the ride."

My vision doesn't seem right. I blink several times, trying to regain my focus, but it only gets worse. Vibrant colors begin to invade my peripheral. Beautiful pinks, blues and greens. The crashing of my phone hitting the pavement catches my attention briefly, until I am mesmerized by the colors again. Shifting my eyes toward the direction of the color, it pulses away from me. Reaching out I try to grab them. Instead, they evade me.

Laughter echoes behind me. It sounds like it's bouncing off the house and trees. Each individual laugh gets louder as it bounces closer to me. Covering my ears and shutting my eyes, I shake my head, whispering to myself, "Please make it stop."

No matter how tightly I close my eyes, it doesn't stop. The colors are still there. My eyes want to chase them. I stop shaking my head when I start to feel more dizzy.

My body lowers itself to the cold ground, loose rock and gravel crunch beneath me as I kneel. Bringing my body into itself as I slightly rock back and forth.

"Please make it stop. Please make it stop."

Something touches my back, causing me to jump in place.

"Banks, be a good fucking girl and face the consequences of your actions. Your recent choices are now defining how you spend the rest of the semester. But most importantly, the next two weeks."

A deep voice taunts me. Even with my hands covering my ears, I can hear him clearly.

"Banksy, welcome to hell."

CHAPTER 8

LANDON

The chick is tripping balls. Maybe we dosed her a little too much?

It's not like she can overdose on it, Venom is top tier shit and death is not included. This morning Hud filled me in on his little plan.

It's turned into a big fucking plan, actually. A lot of moving parts and with some help from Raiden and Flynn, we have been able to execute part one flawlessly. Trick the bitch here, get her alone in the dark, and drug her with Venom. We liquified it, put it in a syringe and popped it in her neck. Now she is on the ground in a pathetic display, *'make it stop, please make it stop.'*

How fucking embarrassing.

"Bro, it's fucking cold. Open your trunk and I'll toss her in before jumping into her car." Hud barks at me.

Tonight was our only opportunity to do this. Rumor has it she has no family, so Christmas break is the perfect time to do what's in store for Banksy.

My face remains expressionless. I'm disgusted really by what I am witnessing. Weak. She is so fucking weak.

If you are going to fuck us over, you need to be stronger than this. She had to have known consequences were coming.

Without responding, I turn around and make my way over to the Range Rover. Opening the hatchback and turning my cell phone flashlight on, it is casting the only light on this dark property.

I turn when I hear a grunt behind me. Hudson has thrown her fireman style over his shoulder and makes his way over.

"She hasn't a fucking clue what she's in for. If she thinks this is bad..." Hud smiles and starts chuckling. I've not yet seen the basement. He's wanted to keep it a surprise, the guy has been working on it for days. His dedication has been impressive. Only taking periodic breaks for practice, the game tonight, and pussy. After we drop Banksy off, we are heading out to the frat party being held in the team's honor to celebrate our win. It's not like we can do much with her tonight while she's like this. Tomorrow, once she's come down, the games will begin.

Hud throws her in the trunk. Banks' body is limp with her eyes shut as she positions herself in the fetal position. Her body is shaking slightly and her breathing is heavy.

"I'll take her car back to her place. Follow me there. Make sure to turn your headlights off when we hit her street so people don't see you, bro." Hudson turns around and begins walking toward her car whistling.

"Bro, do you have her keys?" I question him.

"She left them in her car, it's fine. Just go." He shouts while waving his one hand in the air. He loves this. Lives for it. This is just the appetizer for him, he's already craving the next course. Needing to see and feel the hurt and pain he is inflicting.

I'm all about the long game. Psychological torture. My play time will come.

"Let's go!" Hud yells before slamming her car door and starting her engine. Tires spin against the pavement as he hightails it out of here. Closing my trunk, I walk around the Range Rover to the driver side and hop in.

Before turning the car on, a small whimper comes from the back, "Can you please make it stop? I don't like this. I'm so dizzy."

Not responding, I shake my head while glancing at her in my rearview mirror. So fucking weak. No one is coming to help you. No one is going to save you.

Following my brother, I peel out of the abandoned manor, keeping my headlights off for about a mile down the road to not draw attention. One set of headlights in, one set out. No questions asked. My hood is still on, which falls slightly over my forehead. Some guys wear hats, I wear hoodies. I'm my most comfortable this way, in the shadows. I get more attention because of it. Chicks like the mysterious hockey player who's into art, gives them a challenge I suppose. I couldn't give two fucks about them. If I need to get my dick wet, I have a rotation of chicks who aren't clingy and don't ask questions. They know what they are good for. No emotions or you're out.

Fuck, I need to pack my machine still. A few guys on the team want some ink done before break. I told them I would hook them up at the party tonight. That shit calms me. The buzz of the machine, needles packing the skin with ink, with art. It's fucking beautiful.

Before I know it we are pulling up on the street where Banks' apartment is. I stop down the street as Hud parks her car in her spot. Once the lights are off, he gets out and casually walks toward me. Unless you were looking for him, you wouldn't notice him. The lights on the street are dim, not at all safe for someone like Banks at night, but it's working to our advantage tonight, so who am I to care?

My passenger door opens and Hudson jumps in, giggling like a fucking school girl.

"Dude. What's so funny?" I ask while doing a U-turn and start driving toward our place a few minutes away.

"Bro, smile. This is so much fucking fun." He isn't one to hide his emotions, so I shouldn't be shocked by his excitement. Shaking my head in response, tiny whimpers come from behind us again.

"She's been like this the whole drive. I've never been stuck in a car with a more annoying person." Hudson laughs at my declaration. Then loud coughing followed by groaning catches our attention. My nostrils flare, "So help me if this chick just vomited her guts out in my trunk. I am not cleaning that shit up. No fucking way, bro."

"Like fuck I'm touching it. I'll get a rookie over to clean that shit."

Looking over at Hud, he already has his phone out and his thumbs are racing against his screen. It's not a bad idea.

"Are you going to tell them some chick threw up back there after sucking your dick?" We are pulling up our street, so I turn my attention back to the road.

"Oh, he jokes!" Hud throws back while putting his shoe clad feet on my dash. He knows I hate when he does it. It's his way of saying fuck your joke, without saying it. He can't fathom a chick being repulsed by him.

Pulling up into our driveway, I park and turn the Rover

off. Still looking ahead of me, "You get her out. I'll meet you inside." He doesn't argue it. His basement of wonders awaits. He can bring her down there, considering I haven't a fucking clue what I am about to walk into. I tried once, but he's kept the door locked. I am not one to question his madness. We both have our idiosyncrasies. Which shouldn't be alarming to anyone, we did share a womb, after all. Getting out of the Rover, I grab the house keys from my pants pocket and unlock the door. I walk further into the house and toward the kitchen, turning the light over the stove on. It's just enough light for Hudson to see where the fuck he is going. Speaking of the devil, the door slams open as I look over my shoulder, "Brother! Let the games begin!"

CHAPTER 9

HUDSON

"Yeah, she threw up good back there. Shit fucking stinks." She did a number redecorating Landon's ride. And I swear to Satan if she gets sick on me next, she will be punished appropriately. I have her thrown over my shoulder as I walk through the house, making my way over to the door that will reveal her home for the foreseeable future. Banks is still bitching and moaning, like the world is ending. She has no idea. It's only the beginning baby Banksy.

Landon throws his head back dramatically, letting out a loud sigh of frustration. We don't have time for his theatrics this evening. Pulling out a key from my pants pocket, I insert it into the padlock I had added to the basement door earlier this week and turn it until it pops open. Leaving the key in it, I twist the base and lift the shackle up and through the metal d-ring attached to the door. Using my other hand, I flip the hinge and place the open padlock back through the metal ring, leaving it hanging there open.

I hear footsteps behind me. Landon hasn't seen what I've been working on. This will be the first time anyone other than me has seen the basement in its new state. Turning the doorknob, I look back at my brother. "Are you ready?"

"We have already drugged and kidnapped the chick. No going back now."

He isn't wrong.

Turning back around, I open the door and flip the light switch to turn on the lights going down the stairs and, in the space below. With each step, Banksy moans. "The colors keep moving away from me. I hate this."

"Fucking amateur," Landon mumbles under his breath. The sound of our footsteps on each wooden step echo down the stairwell until we reach the bottom. Banksy is still slung over my shoulder as I walk toward the middle of the space, turning around in time to get Landon's reaction.

His eyes widen as he takes it all in. I can see him examining each item and the area meticulously.

"When... where did you get all this?" he asks in disbelief. Does the guy forget who the fuck I am?

Laughing at his borderline insulting question, "Bro, it wasn't that hard to source this shit."

He finally looks over to me, "What's the plan?"

"I have a couple cameras set up which feed into phones. The cameras don't record. It's a live feed so we can keep an eye on her when we are out. That—" I say pointing to a shackle, "goes around her throat. It's connected to that metal chain which I secured using that O-ring, which was already secured to the floor. The previous owners must have been into some kinky shit down here. As you can see, that old mattress is her bed. No blankets or pillows. I have covered all the windows down here with glass tint. A classic 'honey bucket' for her to handle her business on, and the stainless cat dishes house her water."

Landon is still looking at me in disbelief. "Bro. I don't know what I expected, but this was not it." This isn't my first rodeo. To this degree, perhaps it is, but ruthless behavior isn't anything new to me.

"Enough chitchat. Help me get her undressed and hooked up would ya?"

Wasting no time, he walks over to her new leash as I bring her over to her new bed. Tossing her down on it, she opens her eyes, "Wow, you're so gorgeous. Can I touch your face?" She asks while looking at me.

Ignoring her, I bend down and slide her shoes off, then her leggings. As I go to remove her hoodie, "Let me help you with this, Banksy." I whisper into her ear, but she says nothing as she allows me to drag it up her body, over her head and her arms being the last out of it. She flops them back down next to her, in nothing more than her black lace panties and matching bra. Landon is next to me, already latching the shackle around her nape, locking it with the small padlock that is on it. The key is in my room. There is no chance she is getting out of it.

Standing up, I grab her discarded clothing and walk them over to the other side of the room where she will be able to see them but not get to them. Landon looks up, watching what I am doing. Without looking back, I put them down. I know he is pleased. The guy is all about the mind games.

Throwing them down in a messy pile and heading

toward the stairs. There isn't much more to do tonight other than put the camera app on Landon's phone and wait for her to sober up.

"Hey, wait here a minute. I have an idea." Landon sneaks past me and takes two steps at a time as he heads up the stairs.

He is quick to return, with his tattoo machine, ink and a sinister grin on his face.

Wasting no time, he pours some black ink into the cap and turns his machine on. Dipping the needles in the ink, he moves the needles toward her, marking her delicate fair skin. Not wanting to ruin the surprise of what he is doing, I pull my phone out seeing a few missed texts from the guys asking where we are. I reply to a couple letting them know we are on our way.

"Did you get rid of her phone?" Landon breaks the silence.

"Yeah, I took the SIM card out and turned it off before leaving the manor. Made sure Flynn had his phone wiped, and there's no evidence of him texting her. Raiden said he and the guys would handle it and wipe any traces of us being tracked there."

My brother nods in response as he continues inking our new houseguest. A few more minutes pass before he leans back on the balls of his feet. I walk toward him and look over his shoulder.

Motherfucker branded her.

A small *L* and *H* are on either side of a larger *C* pushed out in the middle, right on her pelvis.

Landon and Hudson Cooper.

Patting him on the shoulder, "Nice work brother. Let's go, we got a party to get to."

CHAPTER 10

HUDSON

Both of us changed before driving over here, dressed in black jeans, sneakers and hoodies. Landon brought his tattoo machine and ink; some guys on the team wanted a few small things before break. Landon doesn't even charge them. He just loves doing it. His passion is his art. Mine is the game. Hockey primarily, but the game we just started with Banksy is already a close second.

Music is pounding. People yell when we walk in, "Coopers are here!" and cheers ensue. After the brawl tonight, everyone is still pumped. Adrenaline flowing through our veins. Smiling at the crowd, I high five those I walk by, a couple hand me shots, which I slam back.

Landon can't be bothered. He walks to where he normally chills during these things, in the backroom. It's quieter there with booze and drugs and a few of the guys who also can't stand the crowds. I'll party with my fans for a bit before heading back there to join them.

LANDON

My hood is on, with some of my hair hanging over my forehead. I have my machine set up and Smiley is sitting in front of me on the couch. He wants something to commemorate this evening's events, a smiley face around his nipple. His nipple will act like the nose. To each their own, who am I to judge?

"Bro, shirt up." I instruct him. He wastes no time lifting his entire shirt off, sitting back on the couch and rubbing his hands together. I should also mention, this is his first.

"Stay like that and don't move. This will be quick, but it's also your nipple, so not entirely painless."

The sound of the machine buzzing fills me with satisfaction. This is my therapy.

Dipping it in ink, the needles suck it back like my brother is sucking back shots. Leaning into Smiley, I use one gloved hand, to stretch the skin, the other hand holding the machine, which I slowly move over his skin. After a quick line, I lift it up and check in with him. "You good?"

He nods in response. "Yeah, keep going."

And I do. Carefully outlining the circle that goes around his nipple. The machine vibrates slightly in my hand. The buzzing centers my mind, tuning everything else out around me. My entire focus is on what is happening here and now with my machine, needles, ink, and art.

Grabbing more ink into the needles, I start on the eyes and mouth. All of it quick work. Easy work. But it's my work, and it needs to be perfect.

When the last line is done, I sit back and examine my work, making sure everything is up to my standard. Which it is. The guy didn't move once. He is one tough SOB.

"And you are done." I tell him as I put my machine down and grab the cleaning solution and paper towel. I clean off his new addition, then finger off my gloves. He stands up, while looking down, admiring it.

"Fuck. This looks sharp. Thank you," Smiley slaps my shoulder.

"Glad you like it, man."

He was my last one of the evening. I did a couple other guys before Smiley. Small shit.

Cleaning up my area, I toss the needles, ink caps and other shit I've used tonight. Wipe off my machine and pack it up in its case.

It is perfect timing because that is when Katie walks in. And where Katie is, there are drugs.

"Landon. I heard you had your machine here. I'll have to get one from you next time," she says when she sees it's been packed up already.

I just sit and look at her, waiting for what she has to offer us.

"Alright Ms. Katie, show us your goodies," Barlowe winks, flirting with her. Katie knows better than to fall for his charm.

A baggy of white powder drops onto the table. Christmas has arrived early. Snow has landed.

Cocaine. Barlowe is the first to jump in. Grabbing the baggy and pouring some of the powder onto the coffee table in front of us. While he is doing that, I grab a card out of my wallet and start cutting it. Dividing it up into a bunch of lines for us.

Katie, being a team player, passes Barlowe a rolled up dollar bill first. He places it into one nostril, plugging the other and quickly snorts his line. Sitting back, his feet lift, "Woo. That shit is good!"

Removing the bill from his nose, he shakes his head a few times. It must sting because his eyes water a bit. Passing it to me, I do my own line and, it burns going up my nose and into my brain. Tingles of numbness encompass me. I feel on top of the goddamn world.

The others take their turn. This shit is next level.

"This has got to be more than just snow?" I question Katie.

She nods, "Yeah, I threw in a tiny bit of Venom. Still gives you the same high as cocaine with an added kick."

And that it does.

"Brother! What do we have here?" Hudson storms into the room, wasting no time. Looking over at him, he clearly just got fucked. His hair is a mess, zipper undone, with a flushed face.

"Don't know her name. Don't care about her name. But my dick thanks her pussy for her service." I sit back, laughing at the guy. Sometimes he is a complete dick about it, others it's like the best fucking time.

He sits down next to me, and pulls out his phone. I glance over and see what he has on his screen.

Her.

It's been hours since we left her. Banks is tossing and turning, which means she must be coming down from her high. I need to be home to see her face when she wakes up. I need it forever embedded in my mind. The shock, the slight bit of hope of seeing me standing there, then her absolute disappointment when I walk away, leaving her almost naked, chained, and vulnerable. Her cries for me to come back, to help her. Pleading with me to save her. She will give me whatever I want, if I just let her out.

None of it will work.

Warmth spreads through my body from the mixture of drugs and this beautiful picture I've painted in my mind.

"Lando, where's Raider?" Barlowe questions.

Motherfucker knows I hate being called that.

I stand up and walk in front of him, grabbing his throat, "Don't. Call. Me. That." I say through clenched teeth.

"Wow, bro. Chill out. I was just playing. Sorry man." His body stays relaxed under my touch, not at all affected by my presence.

Giving him a slight nod and removing my hand from him.

"He said he would stop by if he could. Some shit came up." They know what I mean. I don't need to elaborate further. Our guy has a lot of moving parts going on in his life besides school and hockey.

A bunch of giggling and laughter catch my attention by the door where a couple of drunk chicks are stumbling their way into the room, "Uh, hi." They can barely get that out of their mouths without slurring. Sloppy.

Barlowe looks over at them, "And what can we do for you ladies?"

He has a girlfriend, so he has no interest in humoring them either. She isn't about the party scene, which I respect and none of us push for her to be. For us, it's part of the gig.

"Uh, we were hoping... We heard this is where the real party takes place." says a redhead with her tits basically falling out of her top.

"We invite people in here. Not the other way around. Get the fuck out of here before you regret stepping foot in this room." Hudson tells them.

The blonde has some serious balls to talk back to him. "Why is she in here then?"

"She was invited. She is always invited. We like her. We don't like you. So if you were looking to fuck some hockey player, go to the Richardson party. Their team is filled with desperate cocks." Hudson adds without ever looking over to them.

"You guys are mean." Red snarks back.

"And does it look like we fucking care?" I chime in. They are starting to annoy me now. "My brother has already gotten his dick wet tonight. Mine has absolutely no interest in either of you. Barlowe is taken. Smiley here has some standards. Katie may like both cock and pussy, but she is definitely not looking at getting to know either of yours better."

They open their mouths to say something but quickly close them.

Smart.

Then they scurry off like wounded animals.

Katie and Smiley erupt with laughter.

"You guys are savage," Katie says between laughs.

"No point getting their hopes up, babe." Hud says matter-of-factly as I nod in agreement. Katie may suck our dicks from time to time, but the girl is like a step-sister to us. We embrace her as one of ours. She's a cool fucking chick and that shit's rare.

Still standing, I check my phone, it's nearly two in the morning. Looking over to my brother, "I'm outty. You coming?"

"Have a great Christmas everyone. We will see you next semester." We go around hugging the guys and Katie. "Smiley, take care of that shit. Got it?" He salutes me in return. I'm telling you, this guy is something else.

I grab my tattoo machine case and Hudson follows as we head out. It's time to begin our Christmas break fun.

CHAPTER 11

BANKS

I'm so cold.

My teeth are chattering as my body shakes.

I haven't opened my eyes yet in fear that it will only make me feel dizzy again. I've only just stopped feeling that way. My stomach hurts from it, and my mouth is dry and tastes like I have already thrown up because of it. I desperately need some water, and my head feels like it's being pounded on.

I never want to feel this way again.

Deciding to bite the bullet, I open my eyes slowly and one at a time.

It's dark, pitch black. My eyes begin to adjust to it, and I don't feel another dizzy spell coming over me. Taking a deep breath, I can vaguely see what lurks in the dark, but none of it seems familiar.

Where the fuck am I? Rubbing my hand along my face, I realize I don't actually remember much of last night. My face reddens with warmth from embarrassment. This is not me, not who I am. I don't do this.

Pushing myself off the mattress, I place one foot on the floor in front of me, it's freezing and feels like cement. The mattress is directly on top of it. It's no wonder I am freezing. I have to get out of here.

My heart drops. Please tell me I'm not at a student's place right now. A single tear slides down my face, mortified at the thought. I am not this person. What have I done?

Putting my other foot down, I use all my strength to get up, still feeling like shit despite everything racing through my head. Taking a step forward, I hold my hands out in front of me. It's still very dark and I can barely make anything out around me.

On my next step, I hear something rattle behind me. Like the sound of metal clanking together. Turning my head, I see nothing and no one. Not even an outline of a person.

Where is my phone? It has a flashlight. I didn't even think to feel around for it when I was in bed. I just want to find the light switch, get my shit and go. Forget any of this ever happened and hope no one recorded anything. My career would be in ruins.

My hands are still out in front of me, feeling for anything and finding nothing. Where is the fucking wall?

Suddenly, I am jolted backward. Something chokes me, pinching my skin and cutting off my airway, briefly causing me to cough. I cautiously raise my hands up to my throat, afraid of what I will find. Cold steel tingles on my fingertips. I feel around it and find a hanging piece on one side, and try to figure out what it could be. It is also cold, a larger bottom with a thinner piece hooking around... it's a padlock. My eyes widen and my heart races, thumping rapidly against my chest. My hands continue making their way around my neck and as they meet in the middle, I feel it, a chain. As I turn around slowly and take a step back toward the bed I feel the cool metal of the chain links skim across my skin. Goosebumps erupt all over my body and my bottom lip begins to quiver. The fear is setting in. The realization of it all washes over me. I am trapped. No one will notice I am missing until I am due back at work. Whoever has done this to me knows this.

Rubbing my hands over my body, I can feel the lace of my bra on my chest and my panties are still on. My body isn't sore, just cold, which means I don't think I was raped. A wave of relief washes over me. It also doesn't feel like anything else is restraining me, just the chain and shackle around my throat. My feet pad on the cement as I scurry back to where I think the bed is. Stopping just before it, I bend at the knees and place my hands back out in front of me to lower myself back onto it.

I bring my knees up to my chest and hold them tightly to keep my body heat in. I can vaguely hear a furnace ticking before it roars to life, terrifying me. I'm overwhelmed, my senses are struggling to absorb everything. I've lost all sense of time. Squeezing my eyes shut to fight back tears, I try to think positive thoughts.

The sun has to be coming up soon. Things are scarier in the dark. The sun will bring the light. I need the light. I need to have hope.

I need to make it out of this alive.

CHAPTER 12

LANDON

With the night vision cameras Hudson installed, we can see everything our new pet is doing down there no matter the time of day. A grin spreads across my face as I sit at the kitchen table, watching her. She's realized she's not leaving. Right now, Banks is sitting on the mattress holding herself tightly, slowly rocking back and forth.

Pathetic and weak, just as I suspected.

I stand up and lower the black balaclava over my face and get ready to go to the basement. Hudson left the key in the padlock so we both would have access to her as needed. Unlocking it, I slowly begin opening the door. It's four in the morning and the kitchen is dark, so she shouldn't be alerted by any light that might sneak through. Stepping down onto the first step, I turn my body to close the door behind me. Instead of being gentle, I slam it. The loud noise ricochets through the narrow stairwell down to the basement. I hear a small yelp come from the dark.

This is going to be fun.

Wasting no more time, I flip the light switch on and walk down the rest of the wooden steps. Keeping my hands in my pockets, I take the final step and reveal myself to her. Her face goes from hopeful to disappointed. Turning my head slightly, I stay where I am, not moving. I want to see her next move. What will Banks do?

"Why?" she asks softly. Her eyes look sad and her lips tremble as she pouts. I don't say anything back. Instead, I continue to watch her.

She waits a few moments before realizing I am not going to give her what she wants. Help or answers.

Banks takes in her surroundings for the first time. Her eyes squint, still adjusting I assume, as her head moves from side to side, looking around the room.

Biting her lip, her eyes lock on where we put her clothes. A slight bit of hope washes over her. I see it in her eyes. Her posture changes from folding within itself to sitting up straighter and more confident. Banks looks over at me, then back to her clothes. Getting to her hands and knees, she crawls over to them. The chain links tap each other as she moves, creating a clanking sound. We purposely put them there. She can see them, but never reach them. Taunting her each time we have the light on. Then haunting her in her dreams when the lights are off. Just as she tries to reach for them, still on her hands and knees, the chain stops her. Yanking her back slightly.

"No, no, no," she mutters under her breath.

All hope leaves her eyes as she maneuvers her body in

an effort to reach them. From reaching her fingers as far as she can to pivoting in place to reach with her legs and feet.

Her palms slap against the cement flooring. Banks' head hangs in defeat, realizing she won't ever be able to reach what she desires as long as she is shackled and chained.

I'm still standing in place, observing her. Interested in seeing what she will do next. *Come on Banks, surprise me.*

"Stop just standing there watching me!" She shouts at me. I don't respond. She is looking for a reaction she will never get.

Then she roars to life. Standing up and charging right at me.

What a fucking child.

She is full of determination. I will give her that. Determined and stupid.

Before she can reach me, the restraint jolts her back with force, causing her to stumble backward, but she doesn't fall, which is mildly impressive.

"I hate you. I'm not going to beg you to let me go. People will be looking for me. It's Christmas!" Should I call her bluff now or make her think I have fallen for it? Decisions, decisions.

"You have no idea who you've messed with." She spits out. I bite the inside of my lip to stop myself from laughing. Not wanting to give away who I am just yet. But her bullshit is getting out of hand.

Shaking my head at her only seems to piss her off even more.

"You motherfucker! You'll regret this." The words leave her seething mouth with such hate, it turns me on ever so slightly.

"You can at least give me a blanket, and maybe some water." Now she is demanding shit. The balls on this girl. Again, I am even more impressed. Banks is full of surprises.

Is this backbone real or just for show? Time will tell.

I nod toward her water bowls, and she follows my gaze.

"You have got to be kidding me."

I am absolutely not.

Turning back to face me, she pleads, "What about a blanket? Please, I'm freezing down here." Her eyes are so expressive. Flipping quickly from hope to determination to shock and denial. I only shake my head no in response.

And there it is. Defeat. Her eyes are the key to her mind, her thoughts, her emotions. She can't hide anything from me now that I know this.

Now it's time to surprise you, Banks.

I keep my eyes on her when I slide a hand out of my pocket and move it behind my head. She looks back at me inquisitively. Once I feel the brush of hard plastic, I use my index finger to flick it downwards. The room is plunged into darkness immediately.

Blinking my eyes, allowing them to adjust, I can see her silhouette. She hasn't moved from where she stood in the light.

"Please, don't leave me down here. Not in the dark," she begs.

Worthless.

Walking toward her, I keep enough distance so she cannot reach out and grab me. I am in control of this game, not her.

Her heavy breathing fills up the silent space. She is nervous. Good. She should be.

I reach out and grab her chain, pulling her backward. A choking sound comes as I force her to walk backwards. I can only assume she is reaching at her metal collar, trying to create space between her throat and it.

Wrapping the chain around my fist the closer she gets, my hold only tightens further. Banks is in front of me, and

I yank on the chain once more, forcing her onto the bed. A yelp leaves her. I remain quiet. Still not giving anything away.

She coughs a few times as I keep my hold on her chain, giving some slack so she's no longer being choked.

"Why? Why are you doing this?" Her voice is raspy.

Bending over, reaching my other hand out, I grab her face, squeezing her cheeks and chin between my grip.

I move my face closer to hers. When she feels my presence, Banks tries to inch backwards, but I hold her steady in place.

Don't fight it, little girl, it will only make things worse for you.

Her body begins to shake with fear of the unknown. What will he do next? Worst-case scenarios must be running rampant through her pretty little head.

Lucky for her, none of that will happen to her tonight... yet.

Her scent is pure. Vanilla with a hint of pear. Exquisite. Innocent. Naïve.

My tongue connects with her chin. I slowly move it up her face, tasting the salt from her tears on her cheek. As I reach her forehead, I pull back slightly as she tries to speak.

"Please, don't do this. Please."

It comes out mumbled as my hand still is squeezing her face. I bring my lips to hers, kissing her quickly and aggressively. Biting at her lip before pushing her head away and letting go. The force causes her head to hit the mattress. I hear rustling next. I can only imagine she is in the fetal position trying to protect herself.

Protect herself from what she thinks is coming next, but it's not.

Standing up, I turn on my heels and walk back to the stairs. Not looking back at her when I hear more whimpering from behind me.

Taking the stairs two at a time and reaching the top in no time at all, I flick the lights back on with the switch located up here. She is not going back to sleep. Banks will be tortured by her clothes sitting so close yet so far away. She will be tortured not knowing what will come next.

Lifting the mask off my face, I leave it bunched up on my head, opening the door and closing it again behind me as I enter the kitchen. I relatch the lock and make sure it is securely locked.

"Did you have fun with our guest, brother?" Hudson asks from the dark.

"You know I did."

He chuckles at me, "It looks like she did too."

Turning around, the glare of his phone shows me he is leaning against the countertop. Then it goes dark. I don't say anything more, grabbing my phone off the table where I left it, then leaving the kitchen and heading up the stairs to my room. Hudson's footsteps follow me up. I enter my room and close the door, leaving the sound of his footsteps behind me.

A loud scream echoes through the vents.

I can hear Hudson laughing hysterically.

She is so fucking dramatic. Nothing has even happened to her yet. She screams once more before stopping. Good fucking girl, no use wasting your energy. No one is coming to save you.

CHAPTER 13

BANKS

The lights have been on for what feels like hours. The windows are tinted, making it hard to tell if the sun is up yet or not.

I've tried to sleep to pass the time until my new friend returns to continue my torment, but my mind has been racing. Between that and the lights, sleep hasn't come easily. I've been racking my brain. This has to be a case of mistaken identity. I have absolutely no idea why someone would want to do this to me. There is no reason why I should be here right now. What the fuck happened at the fire last night?

I remember pulling up to the Manor and snooping around. After that, nothing. Everything fades to black.

My head is pounding. I squeeze it tightly at my temples, helping to relieve some of the pressure. Then I remember the water bowls left for me like I am some sort of pet. Rolling over on the bed, I crawl toward them. I am so fucking thirsty.

Tears well in my eyes as I look down at them. This is so degrading, but what other choice do I have?

Picking one up, I bring it to my mouth but instead of drinking it back like a cup of water, I slurp it, not wanting to risk wasting a drop. The water is cold against my tongue and refreshing as it soothes my parched throat. Before I get too carried away and drink it all, I stop myself. Unsure of when I will get more, I don't want to drink it all and then have nothing for who knows how long. Putting it down, a thought enters my mind. What happens when I need to use the restroom? Looking around the room, I spot a tall bucket equipped with a plastic seat with the words 'Honey Bucket' decorating the side and a roll of toilet paper next to it, giving me my answer. I'll have zero fucking dignity left once I use it. Tears well in my eyes when frustration and the feeling of helplessness rush through my body.

I don't understand why this is happening.

Crawling back to bed with my chain following me scratching along the cement makes me wonder, what is this thing connected to?

My eyes follow where it goes, trailing behind me then wrapping around the top of the bed to the other side where it is connected to an O-ring secured to the floor. Getting up, I scurry to the O-ring and try to yank it free. It is attached to a small, thick metal plate which has four screws going into the ground. I pull it a couple more times but nothing gives. My effort is useless, but at least I tried. Feeling even more defeated I go back to the bed and lay with my back toward the stairs, hiding my emotions from him should he come back down. People like him only feed on this shit and I am giving him exactly what he wants.

HUDSON

I'm letting her sweat a little.

It's mid-afternoon before I decide to pay Banksy a visit, bringing her a pb & j sandwich, a banana, and a bottle of water. As much fun as it was watching her slurp water from those dishes these past few hours, murder is not on the agenda. She'll need food and water to survive. We just want to play with her a little. Teach her a little... ok, a big lesson for fucking us with Coach and keeping the money. Did she think we wouldn't notice? That we would just let this happen and there wouldn't be any consequences? And this is who is supposed to be advising us, the team, helping us maintain our grades. Fuck me, we are all screwed if she is the one responsible for our future.

I walk down to the basement with the lights still on, making it easy to navigate. Landon is still in his room, sleeping, I assume. Bro was up late playing with our new friend.

"Good Morning, Banksy!" I shout as I come down the last step.

Her back is facing me, but her head jolts up when she hears me. She must recognize my voice. She flips herself over to look at me, hope filling her eyes, and her voice becomes frantic.

"Oh my god, Hudson! You have to help me."

Then she looks at me. I mean, really takes me in and sees what I am holding in my hands. Her brows raise. "What... I don't... I don't understand," the words faintly leave her mouth.

Not responding, I walk closer to her and slide the plate, banana, and water toward her. She doesn't move. Frozen in disbelief.

Yes Banksy, I won't be helping you anytime soon.

"Think about what you've done. Then you will understand, won't you?" I tsk at her while shaking my finger. Her face scrunches, as if she is dumbfounded. Completely oblivious. This little act of hers will only last so long. Turning on my heels, I make my way back upstairs, turning the lights off before closing the door behind me.

Grabbing my keys off the table to my matte black Mercedes E-Class, I take off. I have a few things I need to pick up for later. Oh, Banksy, your world is about to fall completely apart.

I throw the black plastic bag over my shoulder when I get out of the car and head into the house. Landon is sitting on the couch in a pair of sweats and a t-shirt, with the television on. The patch work ink that decorates his arms on display.

I stand there watching and waiting. It only takes him a second to feel my eyes on him before he turns his head to look at me

"Have you gone down there yet?"

He shakes his head in response.

I wave the bag in front of him like bait. "Well, what are you waiting for?"

He smiles and gets up, leaving the television on. Jerking his head at the bag, "What do you got in there?"

"Oh, just a few things that will make Banksy regret some of her recent life choices."

I go down the stairs with Landon following behind me, it's still dark and I can hear the chain rustling with her movements. When I switch the lights on, Banks is looking directly at us, sitting on the edge of her bed.

Her eyes go to Landon, then back to me. It takes her another minute before it all comes together for her.

"No... Is this all because of earlier this week? All over fucking bag skating? You can't fucking do this to people!" While she's shouting, she stands and walks toward us as much as the chain will allow her.

"That's where you are wrong. We can and we are. And this is so much bigger than just bag skates. You stole from us. You stole from us and then fucked us over. So now it's our turn to fuck you over, Banksy." Spitting the words out in her face. The audacity of this chick.

"I didn't steal shit from you! What are you talking about?" Banks throws back at me.

"Don't fucking lie to me. Don't act stupid and innocent. I see you. We see you for exactly who you are." Landon gets in her face, his hand grips her by the neck, over the collar.

With his hand still gripping her, he walks her back until her ankles hit the mattress edge. He pushes her down onto the bare mattress with some force, enough to where she bounces slightly before laying still. Banks' chest is heaving. She's scared and trying not to show it, but we can see right through this little girl in front of us.

Walking up behind them, I drop the bag and climb on top of her, sitting on her pelvis. As she wiggles beneath me, my warm blood travels south. She is so fucking hot at my mercy.

"In the bag you will find some handcuffs, pass them

to me. I instruct my brother. He wastes no time getting them out and passing them to me. I have Banksy's tiny wrists held tightly in my hand, holding her arms over her head. Her breath tickles my skin as I wait for Landon to secure her.

He wraps the cold, shiny metal around one of her wrists, then the other. Squeezing them both tight until he is sure that she won't slip out of them. Before I can even speak, he is back in the bag, pulling out two zip ties. He slips them in her cuffs and secures them through the chain attached to her collar, which he has made as tight as he can by bringing the excess slack toward us. This way her arms are stuck above her head, unable to move.

Satisfied that she's secure, I let go of her slowly, my fingers trail down her exposed body and goosebumps form, "This shit gets you off, doesn't it Banksy?"

The bag rustles some more, holding my hand out and not breaking eye contact with her, "Pass me it."

He does so without hesitation and places the handle in my palm. Wrapping my fingers around it, my focus now is Banksy and her reaction.

"No, no, no!" she screams, her face is flushed red and her hips buck against me, trying to get me off of her.

"Bro, where the fuck did you get one of these?" Landon's voice is a mixture of shock and impressed.

"Banksy, do you know what this is?" I ask her while holding it up to her, examining as the light glares off the reflective stainless steel.

"You don't want to do this. Please, no, don't do this." She whimpers under me.

"Oh, I very much want to do this. Don't let my charismatic personality fool you. They call me the Spawn of Satan for a fucking reason." A large grin forms on my face. "Landon, hold her legs down, I need her to stay still for this shit."

I feel the bed dip behind me as he positions himself.

"This, Banksy, is a skin graft machine. Some people I know were able to get their hands on this for me. It was freshly acquired for us today, so don't worry it's sterile. Well, as much as it can be in that bag. You are the first one to use it and we start today." I smile at her, and turn it on. The buzzing sound of the machine fills the room as it vibrates slightly in my hand. Banksy continues to squirm under me. Which does nothing to help the hard on I have been battling since straddling her.

I've let my brother tattoo me a few times, but never the ribs. He always says the people he ink's there can barely take it, a few have even tapped out.

Naturally, that's the first place I go on her petite frame. The grafter will only take a thin layer of skin off of her with each stroke of it against her body. There are settings for different thicknesses, which I can control. Today, we are only going with the thinnest option.

Touching the machine to her skin, she screams loudly into the empty space, as the sharp blade begins to cut at her soft, delicate skin. Slowly, I move it down the side of her body, smiling in satisfaction. I am absolutely entranced. As I finish my first graft, I look back at my brother, "Shove your sock in her mouth, we can't have people hearing her."

Landon gets up taking one of his socks off, rolling it in a ball and shoving it in her mouth, stopping her moans and wails of pain. Tears stream down her cheeks and her face is beet red.

Once he is done, he moves back to hold her legs down behind me. The machine is still buzzing as I go in again, taking another graft from the thin skin covering her ribs. At least now her howls are muffled and I can concentrate better as I begin grafting another thin piece of skin off of her. Another rectangular patch begins to show, tiny spots of red blood fill the area. What I am taking is thin enough that blood doesn't come pouring out with each cut. Raising the machine off of her, I leave that piece of skin with the other on her stomach. Shit's kind of gross, even for me. The ultra-thin, almost translucent skin reminds me of when a sunburn begins to peel.

Banks is still trying to fight it and the tears continue to roll down her cheeks. Her face has gone from bright red to white as a sheet.

Noticing her change in complexion, I probably don't have much time before she passes out. We can't have that. She will feel the pain. The agony.

You don't steal from us. You don't fuck with us.

Placing the machine back up to her skin, I pull one more graft before putting her out of her misery. Again she screams, her body moves trying to escape the pain. The attention needed to do this and the extreme focus calms me. It's sort of like hockey. Keep your head up, never lose sight of the puck. The moment you put your head down, you are fucked. This is completely different, but also the same. Keeping my head up and never losing sight or control of what I'm doing. This shouldn't be as relaxing but it is. With each pull I feel satisfied with what I have done. Like people who have the uncontrollable need to press buttons. The release of serotonin gives us the feeling of complete satisfaction.

Maybe this is why dad did what he did, his extreme control. His incessant need to watch everything. Know all. Be everywhere without actually being there. Could this be the same effect it had on him?

Fuck that. I am not thinking about that fucker while I am here enjoying myself. While my dick is hard rubbing against Banks, practically naked, chained and at my mercy.

This image will be engraved in my brain for years to come. It's fucking stunning.

She bleeds for me. Because of me.

"This didn't need to happen today, Banksy. It really didn't. But you did this. You put yourself here."

Lifting the machine up after the final drag, I turn it off and place it down. Grabbing the black bag beside me, I pull out some saline solution and gauze. I pour the solution over where I have just grafted, to make sure it doesn't get infected. I'm not looking for a murder charge. Just a little fun during the holiday season. Once I have doused the area, I add the gauze on top then cover with medical tape, securing it in place.

Looking up at her, I notice her bottom lip is shaking. She's going into shock. Motherfucker.

Tears still stream rapidly down her face. I pull a package of glucose tablets from my pants pocket, open them up and remove the sock from her mouth, "Landon, can you open the orange juice from the bag."

He hasn't said a word this entire time. Instead, he let me enjoy this moment between her and I.

Taking two tablets out and putting them in her mouth, Landon passes me the juice and I pour some in her mouth, "Swallow, these will help." She listens, taking the pills and juice back. I grab a couple painkillers from the same pocket and slip them into her mouth and tell her to swallow again. She listens without hesitation.

Landon remains quiet. Still taking everything in.

Before standing up, I take the grafted skin off her stomach and throw them into my bag, then tie it off. I'll leave the first aid supplies here, we will need to come back in a few hours to change her bandages.

"Keep her cuffed. I'll watch her on the feed. She shouldn't go into shock after what I gave her." I instruct my brother.

Looking down, I admire my work, then glance to the brand my brother left, the *HCL* inked on her lower hip.

My cock is pressed against my pants, hard as a goddamn rock, while admiring our work. I do nothing to hide it, I'm not ashamed.

Now she has two brands to admire from her time here. To always remember what has happened here in the last twenty-four hours, and how she made us do this.

We are Coopers. We are our father's sons. We may not be proud of being his kin, but with the last name comes a vast knowledge base on how to punish those who force our hand. And Banksy, you have fucking forced it.

CHAPTER 14

LANDON

My room is pitch black. Curtains drawn shut, not allowing the rising sun to peek through. Just how I like it, how I *need* it. The silence may not bring peace to all, but it brings it to me. Surrounded by nothingness is calming to my mind.

It's the morning of Christmas Eve. It has been a couple of nights since the skin grafting. We decided to let her heal a bit before continuing with her punishment. We've taken turns going down to feed her and tend to the open wounds. This has made her feel more comfortable with us, more trusting. While Hudson lives for inflicting pain and seeing the reactions immediately, this is where I shine. The long game. The smarter game, in my opinion, although my brother would disagree.

My body is a clock that won't ever let me sleep in. It's almost eight am and I'm laying in bed wide awake. Blowing out a breath of frustration, I roll out of my black silk sheets in only my black boxers, my inked torso on display. I don't have a lot of ink, but the ink I do have, I have done myself. Art is a calming place for me; the pencil drawing along the paper, or the ink from the needle marking the skin. I lose sense of time when I'm creating, minutes quickly turning into hours. It's a beautiful thing.

Sliding on a pair of black sweats, I head out of my room, walking down the hall and stopping at the linen closet. Opening it, I grab a thin white folded sheet and a smaller square pillow, placing both under my arm. I head downstairs. There's no sign of life, which means Hud is still passed out upstairs. We have to make an appearance at *Daddy Dearest's* house today. It's a few hours away, so the later we leave, the less time we have to spend there. That house is nothing but bad memories. Hud would give our father exactly the reaction he was looking for each time. A reason to punish. I think that's where I learned about the long game. Not immediately reacting, how to play mind games. I suppose that is the one and only good thing gained from being raised in that house.

We left the light on in the basement all night, and there's a sliver of it peeking under the door. I grab a bottle of water from the fridge, then the mason jar of overnight oats I made from the counter, along with a spoon I head into the basement.

Easing my way downstairs, I can hear the chain from Banks's movements. She's not been to sleep yet, from what I can gather. I checked the cameras periodically throughout the night and her eyes were open every time. Hudson hasn't noticed, but I am keeping the lights on all night and off during the day. Completely fucking with her sleep schedule.

Last night, I also added some death metal to her nighttime routine. I can hear it still playing from the portable speaker.

Taking the last step, my bare feet make contact with the cold concrete, and a chill runs up my spine. Turning my head, her eyes make her look like a wounded animal, a victim begging for help. Letting all her cards show, she's ripe for the taking.

Bending down, I turn off the speaker. Still keeping my eyes on her.

"Hi, Landon." The pathetic whimper leaves her dry and chapped lips. I ignore her and continue walking toward her. The leftover gauze and first aid cream sits next to her on the floor. Taking in her small frame still in only her bra and panties, I place the water down before her and pass her the oats and a spoon. "Eat."

Her sad eyes widen as her excited fingers reach out, taking it from me. She wastes no time inhaling the food. She is tiny and cannot afford to lose any more weight. Hud made fun of me the other night when I started doing this, but I don't want to malnourish the girl, I only want to teach her what happens to bad, thieving little girls who can't just shut up and do what they are fucking told. I watch in disgust as Banks shovels the food into her mouth. I am not even sure she is breathing between bites.

She looks up mid-bite. "Sorry. I'm so hungry. This is incredible. Thank you, Landon."

Still not caring, I don't respond.

A few more minutes pass, Banks places the jar on the ground with the spoon inside and takes a sip of water.

Her small voice breaks the silence. "Is that for me?" her chin slightly motions to the sheet and pillow still tucked under my arm.

Her collar looks perfect around her neck. Shifting my eyes from it back to her, I take a step forward and hold them out for her to take. She does it swiftly. Throwing the pillow on the bed behind her and unfolding the sheet, wrapping it around her.

"Thank you," she says, tears welling in her eyes.

"It's so cold down here, thank you Landon. You are a good person. You don't need to be doing this with your brother. You are better than this. I know you are." She pleads, thinking she can somehow change my mind. She can't.

When I take a step forward, her body trembles with fear. Nothing good has happened to her when we get close enough.

Taking a seat next to her, and placing my elbows on my knees and face in my hands, I keep her on edge.

Turning my head slightly, "We didn't plan for this to happen, Banks. You forced our hand."

She looks back at me puzzled, confusion fills her face as she continues cuddling the sheet wrapped around her. "What do you mean?"

Rolling my eyes, "You took from us. You stole a lot of fucking money from us, then snitched to coach about our grades." Her face shifts, like she is thinking, then the lightbulb goes off.

"No. I didn't know. I still have it. Let me out, I will go get it." She stands as she speaks.

Not going to happen.

"Sit down. You're not going anywhere, anytime soon."

I can see the defeat spreading across her face, the tears are back.

"That money was to go out to our professors and a portion of it was also for you. They pass us. You keep your

KINSLEY KINCAID

fucking mouth shut, and we all continue with our lives. I even divided it up for you so you wouldn't have to. But you couldn't do one simple thing that could have prevented all of this." My voice is calm as I lay it out for her.

"I didn't know. Let me fix this. I'll give them the money. I can tell Coach I messed up. Please, Landon, let me fix this. Let me leave," she pleads. She thinks by saying my name it will humanize the situation, but it doesn't.

"It's done, Banks. If we are getting punished, so are you. When this is all over, I do expect to get our fifteen grand back. You will get more envelopes under your apartment door for exams and midterms. You will disperse them, the professors will be expecting them. We will pass with flying colors, which we normally did—until this semester. You will not get a cut, you will just fucking do what you are told for once."

Her lip quivers as more tears slide down her fair skin.

"Take your punishment. Stop showing so much weakness. Hudson feeds off your reactions. This will be over before you know it." I try to explain, "Him grafting you, your screams were like music to his ears. You fighting him to get off? It just got his dick hard. Stop reacting and the pain won't last as long."

Another light goes off in her head, "Why can't you just let me go? I won't tell him you helped me. I'll say I escaped on my own."

Shaking my head, "It doesn't work that way. You fucked me over, too. I won't betray my brother. But listen to my advice, ok?" Lifting one hand, I use my thumb to wipe her cheek, and she leans into my hand, closing her eyes. A tiny grin appears on her face. "Thank you, Landon."

Not understanding what she means, I don't respond. Instead, I let her skin touch my hand for a minute longer.

Pulling back, her face tries to move with me but I don't

let it. "We will be gone overnight, we have to go to our dad's. It's Christmas eve. And before you start babbling bullshit, we already know you have no one. There is no one looking for you." She frowns at my bluntness.

"I will bring you more food and water before then. It should last you until morning. We won't be gone long. Cameras will be on. We will be watching, so don't do any stupid shit. If you try, whatever happens after, you caused it. Not us."

Banks nods once, understanding what I am saying. "Thank you. Don't worry I'll be here when you get back. I don't even know how to get out of this," she whispers in defeat.

Before I stand, I place my hand back on her cheek, then bring my lips to her forehead and kiss her. She leans into it. Needing it more than I do.

A slight tingle builds the longer I stay connected to her.

Pulling back slightly, I whisper, "Good girl." Her eyes look up at me with hope.

Pathetic, really.

As I stand, I reach in my pocket and pull out the chapstick I always have on hand and give it to her.

She smiles up at me, and I smile back. Her green eyes are a mix of emotion, but the most important one to me is the tiny bit of hope she is letting shine through.

CHAPTER 15

LANDON

We are still an hour away from our dad's house. It's late, the sun set a while ago and he is going to be pissed we missed dinner. We don't care, but we will hear about it. Words will be had.

As soon as we are done with college, we will be out from under his thumb and finally free.

No longer relying on his finances, we can cut ties and do whatever the fuck we want. Hudson has a bunch of teams wanting him, he will be set. I'll continue with my art. I have enough money saved in a secret account that my dad doesn't have access to, so I'll be fine. We will both be fine and free. I can fucking taste it.

Bro, have you decided if you'll go overseas or just sign with a team straight up?" He hasn't talked about it lately.

"The million dollar question. I don't know. I just want to sign and play somewhere. I don't know where, but I know I have to decide soon. Fucking annoying. This one decision determines the rest of my life, yanno?"

He really does seem like he is struggling with it, but I don't blame him. To decide the rest of your life at twenty-one. Fucking insane. Imagine being eighteen and entering the draft. The pressure and expectations have to be unbearably stressful.

"No, I get it. You know I support you whichever way you decide." I reassure Hud. He is rarely this vulnerable. I don't want him to regret talking to me about it, so I won't pursue the conversation any further.

The gates open and we make our way up the long driveway lined with tall hedges.

"I still can't believe you gave her a blanket and pillow. Fucking pussy." Hud laughs at me. He is watching the cameras again. Guy is addicted to them. So am I. But he doesn't need to know that.

Being here does more to me than I am willing to admit. This house of horrors was our real life childhood nightmare. Barely anywhere was safe inside these walls. I think it affects me more than Hudson. Scars are deep in both of us. Scars I refuse to acknowledge. If our dad saw how I have hidden them, he would only cause more to be

The Rover is parked in front of the door, and we sit in silence.

"Dude, let's go. Old man is itching to tell us off. Let's not delay it." He's right. The longer we wait, the worse it will be.

We get out, and head inside this monstrosity. It is cold and quiet when we enter. The atmosphere is… uneasy. Our shoes creak along the dark hardwood floorboards with every step. The decor is dated, dark green paint lines the walls, with hideous painted family portraits on either side as we walk through the large entrance. A grand staircase is off to the side, leading to our bedrooms. But that is not where we are going now.

"Get your fucking asses in here. NOW!" Daddy dearest shouts from his study down the hall. Both Hud and I roll our eyes and mouth 'fuck'.

The double doors to his study are open, and we walk in side by side, united.

"Do you little shits think it's funny being three hours late for dinner?" Father is leaning against his desk, legs crossed at the ankle, and a glass of whisky in hand. The wood fire is lit, giving off the only bit of light in the room.

We stand before him, not saying anything. He wants a response.

"And you show up looking like slobs. Holes in your jeans, baggy sweaters and sneakers. You know the fucking rules. When you walk in this house you look like a Cooper! Take them off."

We both remain still.

Father's face reddens. Nostrils flare. His bushy salt and pepper eyebrows furrow.

He throws his drink in my face. I do not flinch.

From the corner of my eye, I see Hudson's balled fists. Don't do it brother, I plead with him in my mind.

"Come on Hudson, hit me, I know you want to." He taunts my brother.

He picks on me to get to him.

"No sir, I will not hit you," Hud says through clenched teeth.

Drops of the amber liquid fall off my chin onto my hoodie. I don't dare wipe it away.

"Take the sweaters off. You will look somewhat respectable in this house. Not wearing this shit, being three hours late. Do you forget who pays for your lives? Do you forget the deal we made when I allowed you both to attend fucking Groveton to chase pucks and color fucking pictures?" he spits at Hudson.

"No sir. We are here. We are living up to our end of the deal," I speak up.

"You come home for family meals during the holidays. When you show up, you look like respectful fucking men, not disgusting children! Not only do you look like children, but you are acting like them."

Father walks to the fire, "Take the fucking sweaters off."

Taking a deep breath, we begin removing our hoodies. Both are black and have 'Get Lit' on them with a Christmas tree below. We had these made a couple weeks ago just for today.

Dropping them to the floor, father hears them hitting the ground. Both of us are now just in plain tees. Now we wait for his next move.

Grabbing the fire poker, he sticks it into the flames, "'Get Lit. Get fucking lit." He says to himself.

A few moments pass, and we wait as the tension builds.

Father steps back, poker still in hand, and turns toward us, "Landon, come here son."

I don't move. My heart is racing, but my face remains

neutral.

Father stomps his dress shoe clad foot on the ground. "Get the fuck over here. NOW!"

My feet begin to move, closing the space between us.

"Good. If you flinch, it will only be worse," father explains.

Nodding in defeat, I whisper, "Yes, sir." He always fucking wins and each time he does, I hate him more and more.

The hot steel fire poker connects to the flesh on my arm. Instinct is screaming at me to move it, that it fucking hurts and to just move my arm out of the way. My brain knows I cannot do that. Father pushes into my flesh harder. The smell isn't one you can ever get used to. The sizzling of my own skin makes up part of my nightmares. I can feel my face reddening. But I will not fucking flinch.

He punishes both of us by doing this. As much as this physically hurts me, it hurts Hudson too. He wants to step in, to help me, to protect me. The minute he does though, father will only hurt me more. This challenges Hudson, his urges. He saves all his self restraint for these occasions. Any other time he lets it go, he gets his freedom that way.

A few moments pass before he begins to pull the poker away. My skin is melted on it, I can feel it tug before it unsticks from the poker.

This house always leaves scars.

Not a fucking chance Banks would make it twenty-four hours here. What we have done to her is fucking minor in comparison, if she only knew.

She would be screaming, crying and begging for it all to stop. Feeding into the monster. Banks doesn't have a game face.

And I would never compare Hudson to our father. He is a good person, but if you show any weakness, it is drilled into him to use it against you.

"It won't happen again father," I say, looking him in his eyes. Making it believable as I can. He just nods in response before speaking, "Good. Now get out of my fucking sight."

Turning around I walk back toward Hudson, he grabs my hoodie off the ground for me and we leave fathers study. It went as expected.

Merry Fucking Christmas.

CHAPTER 16

HUDSON

It's Christmas morning,

Although, you would never know it being in this house. Not even a fucking tree is up. If our mom was still around, well, we wouldn't even be in this house. We would be somewhere safe, far away from the devil's lair. It would be decorated head to toe, with the smell of fresh baking and Christmas music.

Mom disappeared one day when we were about eight or nine. It happened around the time father started punishing us more violently. She protested it, tried to fight back and protect us. Then one morning she was gone. We asked questions, but he never gave any answers. It's like she was never here. I will never be like this man when I have kids. I fucking hate him. It wouldn't shock me if we later found out he had our mom killed or hidden her away somewhere. Father owns a bunch of businesses, he is an investor. So his wealth and connections wouldn't make what I think he's done to our mom impossible.

Fuck's sake. It's Christmas, come on Hudson, happy thoughts.

We've finished eating and are sitting in the TV room. No fucking clue what's on the TV, it's more of a background noise as I pull out my phone and check the feeds of Banks. She is up, pacing. Earlier she was doing yoga, to stretch her muscles. Smart girl.

"Mr. Hudson, Mr. Landon, could I get you anything else?" One of the staff comes in and asks us.

Father never bothers showing up for breakfast. He has all his staff in, the bastard couldn't even give them the day off.

Both Landon and I are surprised he hasn't come to gloat.

Landon speaks up first. "No, we are going to head out now. It's a long drive back." The staff member nods and leaves us alone.

"Bro, let's head. He isn't coming down." I say to Landon as I put my phone back in my pants pocket.

He rakes his fingers through his hair. "Yeah, let's go."

Landon's been quiet since last night, processing the events and blaming himself. We are twenty-fucking-one years old and this shit still happens in our lives.

"Dude, it's not your fault. None of this is our fault. Four more months. One more semester, ok?" I reassure him as we stand from the couch.

Walking to the door, we hear footsteps making their way down the stairs.

"Just got word, drug tests your first week back. Don't

fuck up, got it?" Father says with a sharp tongue.

In unison, "Yes, sir."

"Since you boys couldn't make it for dinner, I decided I couldn't make it for breakfast. And to keep the staff on all day. They cannot be with their families today, because of you both and your actions. Learn from this and do better." He scolds us.

"Yes, sir."

It's not our fault. The man is evil and vindictive. The staff knows this. Fuck, he makes me so angry.

Father finishes coming down the stairs, looks at us both, our sweaters waiting for us at the front door, folded on the entrance table. We grab them and go to leave, but he still doesn't speak. It brings an uneasy energy into the room.

We don't feed into it. He's looking for an argument, for any excuse to bring hellfire upon us again. The fucker thrives on it.

He's part of why I am the way I am. Though I would never tell him that. He would love it too much.

The difference is, I know when and where to direct it. The Spawn of Satan nickname came to be in my teenage years, if the glove fits.

We leave without speaking a word, and get into Landon's Rover, still silent as we drive off the property. Crossing through the open gate, a weight is lifted and we both breathe out a sigh of relief.

"How's your arm?" I couldn't check in last night. He still has cameras everywhere, and if he were to see me tending to Landon, he would just do it over it again.

"I'm fine. Nothing I'm not used to. I'll just have to cover this one up once it's healed enough."

He tattoo's over them. He has a few on his chest and torso as well.

Mine are on my back. Anytime anyone has asked, I just tell them I had been in an accident. It's easier than explaining the truth. Poor popular jock gets hurt by his daddy. I am not one to accept a pity party. It's done, it happened. Let's move on, shall we?

Banks needs to learn the world isn't rainbows and butterflies. Her stint in our basement is a walk in the goddamn park compared to what it could have been. I don't feel at all guilty.

"Hud, message the guys and tell them about the drug test," Landon barks at me.

He is rightfully in a mood. I know it's not directed at me, so it's not worth battling over. Pulling out my phone, I send the guys a heads up on our group chat. Raiden is the first to reply, then wishes us a Merry Christmas with the addition of the middle finger emoji. It makes me laugh. He's a nice guy, you could even say he is a charmer.

The text also pops up on the electronic dashboard of the Rover, bringing a smile to my brother's face. He needed that.

We both did.

I will always hate this drive. It better be our last time driving home from that place. We are finally back home in Groveton. It's late, well past sundown and our Banksy needs me, I can feel it.

"Dude, you are way too awake right now." Landon can feel it too, my internal energy is radiating. It's a twin thing. We just know things, feel things. I can't explain it, but it's real.

"Ah, yes, brother. I have plans with Banksy this evening. No need to join me. This will be a one-on-one date." Rubbing my hands together, so many plans and so much time.

"Let me bring her some stuff before you do whatever the fuck it is you're planning. Last I checked, she was out of food." It seems he has taken on the caretaker role.

He can sense it before I even say anything, which I wasn't going to. He had a rough night. I was going to leave this one be... for now.

"You fucker. She has to eat, let it go," he jokes with me. Which impresses me, he was pretty quiet the entire drive back. Being back in Groveton must have him feeling better, now that we are far as fuck away from the sperm donor.

Heading in, I run upstairs to grab a few things and change while Landon hightails it to the kitchen.

LANDON

I kept the lights on the entire time we were gone, but no music. She's gotten used to it, the lights, sleeping for hours at a time while we were away. Now that we are home, I bring her some food and water. Banks rolls over when she hears my footsteps, her dark hair is a mess, her body still covered by the sheet and her face graces me with a soft smile.

"Hey," she whispers to me. I smile back at her. Banks doesn't move when I sit on the edge of her bed, "Here, eat, you need to eat."

She nods as she sits up and grabs the sandwich.

While she eats, I grab hold of one of her feet, and she

flinches at my touch. My thumb rubs the top of her foot in reassurance and that's all she needs to relax again. She should not trust me. She shouldn't allow me to do this to her. As my fingers kneed her foot, massaging them with just the right amount of pressure, a small moan escapes her mouth between bites, causing all the blood in my body to rush to my dick. My jeans are tight enough where she won't notice, but I know, my cock is hard pushing against the fabric of my pants. Placing her one foot down, I grab the other one and repeat while she continues to eat.

"Hud is going to come down and play. He's missed you. Can you be a good girl for him, Banks?"

She swallows loudly, I don't look up to see her face. I already know she is scared. A part of me fucking loves it.

"Landon, I can't. I can't take another grafting. "Her voice is full of panic and sadness. I shake my head, still keeping my focus down on her feet, "He isn't going to graft you again, I promise."

At least I don't think he is. I could be full of complete shit right now.

Her chains rattle when she nods her head, "Yeah, ok. I can handle it."

Placing her foot down, I look up at her. Her green eyes stare back at me, her fear making them shine brighter.

I hold my hand out while still maintaining eye contact, and she passes her empty plate. Setting it down next to me, I lean forward, "Is the collar ok? It's not too tight?"

Her eyes never leave me, her face flushes, "No, it's ok. It doesn't bother me. Well, it's a bit heavy, but not too tight."

My hand reaches up, wrapping around her throat as my thumb sneaks under the metal collar, rubbing her soft, delicate skin underneath.

"Oh my god, that feels amazing," she whimpers.

Still not breaking eye contact with her, her lids are

hooded. She's aroused. If my fingers were to trail down, I am almost positive I would find her pussy soaked.

Before stopping, my lips find her forehead again, and Banks leans into it. Pushing into my kiss. The familiar tingle is back and if I am feeling it, so is she. Letting go of her throat, I pull my lips back and whisper against her, "Be good. I'll be watching."

"I will. I promise, Landon."

CHAPTER 17

BANKS

There is something about Landon. To some, he is mysterious, dark and dangerous. He is sweet, kind and compassionate. I can also sense a tortured soul inside of him. He is only doing what he knows. I have heard the stories of how Hudson is labeled the Spawn of Satan. Everything is for a reason and I would be dumb to ignore that.

The warm gestures toward me make me feel safe. It gives me hope. Human connection is so important, and he is giving me what I desperately miss and need. I just didn't know how much I missed it until now.

He is doing this because he has to. It's all he knows. It's all they both know. This is what I keep telling myself as I wait for Hudson. The feel of Landon's lips against my forehead is something I refuse to let escape me. Hudson is coming, I need this feeling to stay with me while Hudson is here.

Gauze is still on my ribs. Since they left for Christmas, the brothers left me supplies to tend to my newest brand, including packets of gauze, tape and medical cream. They made sure not to leave me anything I could use to escape.

"Oh, Banksy!" I shiver when I hear Hudson's voice.

Nothing can be worse than getting your skin grafted while awake.

Footsteps echo as he marches down each step. My heart is racing. Closing my eyes and taking deep breaths, I tell myself he does this because it's all that he knows. It's because he has to.

My knees are against my chest with my arms holding them as close as possible.

"Banksy, I've missed ya girl," Hudson declares as he reveals himself at the bottom of the stairwell. The guy has energy. It's night and day between him and his twin. "I come with gifts. It wouldn't be Christmas without gifts, would it?"

Seeing nothing in his hands, my interest is piqued while I'm still slightly terrified. His energy is completely different from last time. My nerves are on edge.

"Aren't you curious?" He asks. His brow arches and a cheeky smirk crosses his face.

Taking another breath, "Sure, Hudson. What did you bring?"

"Now that's the spirit!"

He walks closer to me. I fight the urge to move away. To make myself as small as I can so he can't see me. So he will lose interest. But I promised Landon I would be good.

"I was watching the cameras while Landon was down

here. You two get my dick hard. How your body responds to his touch, the way your eyes grew heavy as he rubbed under your collar. That shit was hot."

Denying it would be pointless.

"Lay down on your back. Don't do anything stupid and you will get your present," he instructs as he makes his way over to my bed. I listen, moving myself down the bed so my head is laying on my pillow and I remove the sheet. I may be trapped, but I'm not stupid. He would have removed it for me if I didn't.

Just like the last time, he straddles me at the waist. His fingers gently rub against the spot where he grafted me. "Does it hurt?" He questions with genuine curiosity.

Shaking my head, "No, not anymore. It's itchy more than anything from healing."

Goosebumps erupt on my skin as his finger moves from the gauzed area to my flesh, following the curves of my torso leading to my hips.

"You are at my complete fucking mercy. So fucking beautiful," whispering to himself as he watches his finger trace over my skin, getting dangerously close to my low-rise panty line of the lace.

"Did he show you?"

Confused by the question, he was clearly watching on the feed, "Show me what?"

Shaking his head, "Nothing," is all that he says back.

"These goosebumps belong to me," his eyes move up my body slowly. They stop at my mouth as I bite my lip, wondering what is to come next. He smiles, showing his perfectly straight and white teeth. For a hockey player, I'm impressed he still has all his teeth.

His eyes continue to move again, reaching mine, and we remain like this for a few seconds before he leans forward, hands drop on either side of my head, caging me in.

Hudson's warm breath tickles my skin.

"It's time for your present."

Grinding his pelvis on me I can feel his hard cock pressing up against me. I don't flinch or show my fear or worry. I have to be good. I promised.

Hudson pushes himself back, his strong arms on display thanks to his fitted tee.

Athletes and their arms, need I say more?

Before I realize it, Hudson is on his feet with his hard cock in his hand. His sweats are down below his knees. Precum is leaking from his tip and he casually strokes himself. Taking a few steps forward toward my head, he stops just above me. Tears well in my eyes, fuck.

Nothing gets past him, he chuckles, "Tears don't work on me, Banksy."

He bends at the knees, lowering himself to either side of my head, his tip pushes against my lips, I don't open.

"You will fucking accept your gift and you will like it," he snarks while pushing himself into my mouth.

"Bite me and I will chain your legs spread open so I have access to you whenever the fuck I want. Understood?"

I nod to show I understand. It could be much worse, but as long as I am good, it will be ok. I promised. Landon promised.

Hudson isn't gentle. He forces his entire cock down my throat or as much that can fit. The guy is big. The salty taste of precum paints my tongue as he starts moving himself, thrusting himself back and forth.

His tip slams against the back of my throat, before continuing down, causing me to gag.

"Shh, breathe through your nose," he coaches as drool escapes my mouth.

The tears I was trying to hide begin trickling down my

cheeks.

Hudson leans forward, angling himself so he can get deeper inside of me. He grabs each of my wrists, bringing my arms above my head and squeezes them tightly together.

I continue to gag with each thrust, his movements become more rapid he isn't going to let up anytime soon.

"Fucking take it, Banksy. Take it like the worthless whore you are," he degrades me.

My tongue brushes against the underside of his swelling cock. Hudson's breathing picks up as his orgasm begins to build.

He has my wrists so tight that circulation has been completely cut off, my hands tingle as I try to move my fingers.

This should be over any time now. Please let it be over. I can barely breathe, only little breaths sparingly as he continues his assault on my throat. It's already starting to feel sore. Then, all at once, he lets go of my wrists, and I can immediately feel the blood flow reenter them. Hudson is on his feet, with his hand stroking his cock viciously. It looks heavy in his hand as it continues to swell. I am looking right at it as his warm cum begins to shoot out of it, landing on my face. He doesn't let up, pumping it back and forth as he continues to release himself on me. Some lands on my cheek and forehead before he rasps, "Open your fucking mouth. Fucking take it. I said take it!"

My mouth opens and not to anger him further, I stick my tongue out, ready to catch what's left. More ropes of his warm cum erupt from his head, landing on the tip of my nose then the corner of my lip.

"Good fucking girl, keep that tongue out. You filthy fucking girl."

His movement begins to slow as the last few drops of

cum drip onto my tongue, and he aims his cock using his hand.

"Finish it all. I don't want to see anything left behind on that pretty face," he instructs with his heavy cock now hanging between his strong thighs. Hudson's hands fall to his sides as he watches me. I swallow the drops on my tongue first before using my fingers to scoop up his salty release between my lips. I try to be as seductive as possible to please him.

"Fucking finish it all, Banksy," he whispers, encouraging me.

Taking the last bit from my nose and around my lip, I suck it back. Making a show of it, my chest rises as I look back at him. I make moaning noises of enjoyment as I swallow, "So good, Hudson," I whimper in return.

His hands go to his chest, he rubs himself all the way down his torso before reaching his cock. Hudson rubs his thumb along the tip and bends over on top of me again. His cock is resting on my chin. "Open," he instructs. I do, expecting him to make me suck it off, but he surprises me. Rubbing it along my swollen lips, "Keep it there. Taste me all fucking night." His own chest is heaving, his eyes captivated by his own movements. Then gripping my face with his hand, he whispers, "Merry Christmas, Banksy. This is one neither of us will ever forget."

Then it occurs to me. That is the present. The memory of his assault on me is forever engraved and burned into my mind.

Spit follows, landing in my mouth as he still has my face gripped.

Hudson says nothing as he releases me, slapping my face hard enough you can hear the crack of his palm connecting with my cheek echo through the room. I want to scream. To react like he wants. But I can't, I promised.

He doesn't know better.

Laughing, he rises and pulls his pants up.

"You fucking deserved this. You know you did. Fuck you, Banks Lewis." His eyes are filled with hate and his face screams of disgust.

It's all he says before stepping off the mattress and making his way back to the stairs. He flips the switch at the bottom of the stairwell, turning off the lights and leaving me in the dark. I am grateful. I want to curl up into a ball and cry and wish this would just finally end.

CHAPTER 18

BANKS

I am why I am here.

The cold basement and its distinct sounds are becoming all too familiar now with each moment and day that passes. The creak of the floorboards late at night, or is it during the day? That part I don't know. The clicking sound the furnace makes before roaring to life. And the one tiny mouse that scurries about. It has gotten used to me being here. Any crumbles left behind from my meals and it will come nibble on them. I refuse to give it a name, it makes this real, being chained and tortured in this hell. If I give it a name, it means I'm as pathetic as they think I am. This mouse isn't my friend, it's not my hope or coping mechanism, it's just a fucking mouse.

"What are you thinking about?"

I know that voice, that voice is my hope. He is nothing like his vile fucking brother.

"Nothing important," shrugging my shoulders as my eyes make their way up his beautiful body. He is a student, I shouldn't be looking at him like this. But he is also very much an adult, so it's not like it's illegal. He has a pair of black slides on with his strong bare legs exposed, loose athletic shorts hanging low off his hips. His torso is exposed, the v-line on display near his pelvis makes my mouth water. He has black and gray patch tattoos scattered around his chest. Landon's face is expressionless, making him hard to read. Chiseled jawline with fuller lips and those beautiful blue eyes. His hair is getting too long, it's shaggy and falling over his forehead.

"I can see you checking me out."

I feel my face warm from embarrassment.

"I watched what Hudson did last night. You took it. A part of me even thinks you liked it. Did you like it, Banks? You were such a good girl for me." His praise makes me happy. The last thing I want to do is displease him. Landon Cooper is my only hope.

I nervously bite my lip, but I have to ask, "Hudson mentioned something. Asked me if you showed me?" I feel my body shrink as each word leaves my mouth.

"Ask with confidence or don't ask at all."

I look up to find he's moved right in front of me, so close I can feel his breath. "I understand, you're right."

"Good girl, now ask again."

Mustering up all the courage I can after so many days of feeling nothing but defeat, it takes all the energy I have to sit myself up taller and clear my dry throat before asking again but clearly and with confidence like Landon told me to. "What did Hudson think you showed me?"

Landon sits next to me. "See, was it really that hard?" I shake my head, smiling, feeling proud of myself.

He cups my jaw with his hand. He is gentle with me, the complete opposite of his brother. "Such a good girl for me, aren't you Banks?" His eyes are looking into my soul. It's slightly uncomfortable, but a part of me likes it, *craves* it. Like he can really see me. I am not this bad, vindictive person I have been made out to be. I didn't know what the money was for. I kept it because I thought whoever left it would come back for it. I didn't know.

Landon leans in, his breath tickles my skin while his intoxicating musky scent invades my space. Surprising me, he kisses me softly, his lips on mine. I relax into it. It's gentle, delicate and addictive. The kiss doesn't last long before he pulls back, and I whimper in protest at the loss of his lips against mine. He chuckles softly, raising the corner of his lips and smirking at me, "Patience." Then his hand leaves my face as he turns his body to face me fully. The disconnect is excruciating.

"He was talking about this." He points to what looks like a horrible burn on his left bicep. It's fresh, still red and blistered. It looks like it hurts.

Speechless, I am not sure what to say. "What happened?"

"Don't worry about me, Banks. I'm a big boy and the last thing I care to do is complain about my daddy issues to you." The 'to you' stings. I retreat back into myself, no longer feeling the confidence I did a moment ago. He notices, and his brows furrow. "I didn't mean it like that. Shit, Banks, I'm sorry. It's just that my daddy issues are not something I talk to anyone about." He rubs his chest, specifically the areas covered in ink. As I watch him, something catches my attention, ridges, not large ones, are raised on his skin, like a scar from a cut... or a burn. He catches me looking but doesn't speak, waiting for me to say something. Instead, it's my turn to surprise him. Reaching out, I touch his inked skin and a jolt of electricity spreads through me. Using the tip of my fingers, I trace the scar that his ink is trying to hide, but I see it, I see him. He wasn't born this way, he and his brother were conditioned to be the way they are. Landon's breath hitches as I move from one scar to the next, touching them, acknowledging they are there. They are a part of him and he shouldn't be ashamed. He is strong, he survived and still is.

"Why does he do this?" Looking back up at his face but still keeping my fingers on his skin. His face has changed, like he is in pain. His eyes look away from me as a loud breath escapes him. "Since we were little. Anytime we displeased him, he would teach us a lesson. Kind of like the lesson we are teaching you. As much as I didn't want to become him, it looks like I have, we have."

My hand moves to his face and he flinches at my touch, "Don't say that. This is what you know. This isn't your fault, none of it. Or your brother's."

"Stop being so fucking nice to me; I don't deserve it. You are chained up, almost naked and trapped in our basement. We don't deserve your sympathy. We don't fucking want it either." I tell myself his anger isn't directed at me. It is a defense mechanism. Tears well in my eyes, but I keep repeating it to myself—this isn't personal.

Landon wastes no time, storming up the stairs, stomping with each step and slamming the door. The noise startles me, causing me to jump. I close my eyes, letting the tears escape me. I'm not crying because he was short with me. I cry for him because he won't let himself do it.

This isn't pity. I wish he knew he didn't need to be strong all the time, that it's ok to feel. Being emotional like this isn't normal for me. Being stuck down here with no sense of time or day, being alone with my own thoughts. It's messing with me. The stress, it's the stress of the situation. I can't think clearly anymore. One minute feeling defeated, the next feeling the tiniest bit of hope. Feeling compassion for these two guys. They are why I am stuck down here. But now that I know more about them, I get it. I... I get it and I hate that I do. I hate that a part of me understands why they have done this.

Fuck, listen to me. Caring for my captors. What the fuck is wrong with me?

CHAPTER 19

LANDON

"**Y**ou fucking told her to ask me about the burn?" I shout, barging into my brother's room.

He has some chick on his cock that I've never met.

"A little privacy?" Is all he says in return while the chick keeps bouncing on his dick.

Picking up her shirt from the floor, I throw it at her. "Get the fuck out!" She finally stops, then looks down at my brother, like he will help her. Fucking imbecile.

"You heard him. Get out."

"But I haven't come yet," she whines back at him.

He wastes no time gripping her hips, lifting her off of him and dropping her to the floor, and looking down at her. "What are you waiting for?" On her hands and knees, she gathers the rest of her stuff, gets up and skurries out.

"You fucking told her to ask?" Hud's dick is still out, semi hard. He makes no effort to hide it, not moving from where he lies on the bed.

"Also, since when do we bring chicks back here?" This is not the brother I know. He is fucked up.

"Did she ask?"

"Of course she fucking asked! She saw right through me and knew almost instantly what happened, you fucking moron. Since when do we tell people about our daddy issues?" I fume.

Hudson still isn't phased in the least. "I thought it would be good for you to talk to someone. And she's a chick, so I figured while we have her here, she could help?"

"I don't need anyone's help." I get right in his face, spitting every word. This motherfucker is lucky that's all I am doing.

"What did you do?" he questions back. Retaliation is in our DNA, he is smart to ask, but it doesn't mean I will fucking tell him.

Backing up away from him, I turn around and begin walking out of his room, "I'm going out!"

I messaged some of the guys who were still on campus, asking if there was anything going on tonight. I need to get out and release the anger building inside of me.

Of all the guys fucking Smiley came in clutch. He is at a small frat party happening down the street from the rink.

Fucking perfect.

Throwing my phone down on my bed, I walk to my closet, pulling out a fresh pair of black jeans, a white fitted v-neck tee, and my black and red Jordans. Rushing to put them on so I can get out of this fucking house, that I feel like I am suffocating in.

Looking in the mirror, my hair is a fucking mess, so I grab a black hat and pop it on along with some deodorant and cologne. As I walk out of the closet, passing my desk, I swipe my black zip-up hoodie from the back of the chair and my phone from the bed before heading out.

This chick is getting inside of my head. I don't want her pity. I don't need it. I grab my keys from the dish near the front door and head out.

Pulling up to the frat house, there's a small group of people I don't recognize and, frankly, don't give a fuck about, outside smoking and talking.

Getting out of my Rover, I walk up the brick path to the house and head in. It's a decent size party, which is impressive considering most of campus has fucked off for the holidays.

Maneuvering through students crowding the front entrance, I go looking for Smiley. My eyes continue to scan as I walk past the kitchen and into the living room, where we spot each other immediately. Biggest fucking grin on his face with his hand in the air waving me over to the couch where him and a few others are sitting. The table is littered with empty bottles and drugs.

I've never been a massive drinker. Don't get me wrong, I will have a drink here and there. Getting blackout wasted followed by a bout of dehydration and a hangover never appealed to me, but the drugs have always screamed my name.

The immediate rush of coke or venom filling my body.

Or the calmness weed can bring me. Mixing a few of them together—euphoric. All of it gives me something I need. Something I crave. All without the filthy hangover or night of regret laying next to me.

Standing in front of the couch, I nod my head for whoever this fucker is next to Smiley to move. He does without question. He knows who I am. Good fucking boy.

Rubbing the palms of his hands together, Smiley begins his tour of the goods. "So my man, we have a great selection for you here tonight. Moonshine from bro's grandpa's basement, shit burns, thought I went blind for a minute after taking a shot. So don't say I didn't warn you. Venom, compliments of the Noxious Boys, Merry Christmas to us. And in the dish are some coco puff joints. I know. So many choices."

Shaking my head and smiling, the guy could try to sell me a used condom, and I would buy it. "Bro, drug test when we get back in a couple days. Only Venom. Got it."

His eyes widen like a wave of realization just washed over him. "Fuck dude. I totally forgot. Don't worry, I haven't had shit yet." Jesus Christ, this guy.

Leaning forward, I grab the playing card on the table and cut a line of Venom and snort it directly off the table into my nose. The minute it hits my brain a flashback of the basement invades my vision. Banks.

Banks, almost naked, wrapped in the thin sheet I left her in. My lips touching hers with the zap of electricity traveling through my body. Her innocent body reacted more visibly than mine. Fuck no.

I take another hit.

This bitch will not occupy another thought. She will not feel fucking sorry for me. She will loath me. Hate me. As much as I hate myself after my father's punishments. For being weak. For not having the balls to stand up for my fucking self. Only a few more months and I can. But until then, this is what I have.

Hockey, art and these fucking drugs.

I cut one more line and snort it. My mind tingles as the vibrant colors invade my vision. The music becomes louder, and the beat radiates off other party goers around me.

Now I'm content. This is where I want to be. Zoned the fuck out.

"Raiden and his crew are fucking brilliant, man. This shit, non-addictive and undetectable on drug tests. Fucking brilliant. I need to give him a big kiss at our next practice. He deserves it."

Smiley's voice echoes around the room. I can see it, the purples and blues are bouncing with each word coming out of his low-toned voice box.

Grabbing my phone out of my pants pocket, I throw it on the table. Tonight, I don't fucking care. My head leans against the back of the couch, and my eyes close, taking in this moment of complete bliss. I'm not sure how much time passes before I feel a warm body sit itself upon my lap. My heavy high eyes lift to see it's some random puck bunny blonde who has been following the team around all season. Desperate whore.

As I lift my head, she takes it as an invitation to wrap her arms around my neck.

Before I can shake her away, Smiley catches my attention. He has my phone in his hand. What in the fuck?

"Give it back," I demand sternly. He waves it off like I don't mean it.

Turning to push the bunny off, her lips lock with mine.

"Hey Hud, check this shit out. Your brother's hooking up with the bunny that's been tailing us all season." Is all I hear as my face goes red.

143

I push the chick off me and watch her fall to the floor.

"Don't fucking touch me again!" I stand as I shout at her. Then I look around for my brother, scanning the crowd which has gotten bigger since last time I looked, but I don't see him.

"Down here Lando," Smiley chuckles. He knows I hate being called Lando.

"The fuck are you doing with my phone?"

He flips it around and I see Hudson's face, full of amusement, staring back at me. Motherfucker.

I swipe my phone from Smiley and click the red end button.

"Don't touch my shit and don't fucking call me Lando again!"

Stepping over the bunny, I leave the party. I hear voices behind me calling my name, but I don't bother turning around. My high still lingers but the last two minutes sobered me up a bit.

Motherfuckers.

So much for escaping one reality for another.

CHAPTER 20

HUDSON

We never have chicks over.

My brother never goes to a party without me.

Banks is fucking us up. What the fuck is wrong with us? We need to step this shit up.

Landon just slammed the door shut behind him, making the walls vibrate. The guy is pissed. She's gotten to him. She's under his fucking skin and he let it happen. I know what Landon's been doing with her, the long game. Bro did not anticipate this.

Who am I kidding? Neither of us did. I like playing with my toy, my precious Banksy.

Fuck this.

I didn't even get to finish before my brother threw the chick off me, but to be fair, that shit was hilarious. She had no idea what was happening, then she crawled out of my room with both of us not giving a shit. Fucking gold.

Sighing in frustration, I get up out of bed, put on my boxers, and grab my phone. Heading downstairs, I open the basement door. "Banksy, wakey wakey." My laugh carries down the stairwell, but she doesn't respond. Her chain doesn't even jingle. It disappoints me. Her fear and anticipation is something I have gotten used to since her being here.

"Banksy boo, I am coming to see you."

Still nothing.

Is she gone?

Moving my feet quickly down the last couple steps, I flick the light on and there she is. Her back is turned to me, and she is curled up on the bed with the thin sheet wrapped around her frail body. Banks' black hair is fanned out on the small pillow her head is resting on. Taking her in, I watch as her body rises and falls. The chick is stunning. Laying here at my mercy and completely unaware. My dick hardens, straining against my boxers. Closing the gap between us, I continue to take her in. I softly put my phone down next to me.

I trace my fingers along my torso, tickling the skin, slowly moving down my abs, my flesh raises as I reach the waistband of my boxers. Grabbing my throbbing cock I begin working it. My thumb rubs my tip, feeling the precum dripping out of it. Using my other hand, I shove my boxers down, exposing myself as I grip my cock even tighter. Rocking my hips back and forth, my eyes stay on her. Thinking of her petite frame, and how easy it was to hold her down. To put the grafter against her skin as she screamed and strained against Landon's sock in her

148

mouth. It was goddamn perfection.

My cock swells as I picture it. Her body stirs on the bed, she turns over and the familiar jingle of her chain fills my ears bringing a smile to my face. As her eyes open, I squeeze my cock harder as I continue rocking into my fist. She blinks a few times, adjusting to the light, then focusing on me. Banks doesn't move or speak. Her eyes remain on me and my cock. My abs begin to contract and the familiar tingling sensation rushes down my spine to the tips of my toes as cum shoots out onto her face. Her nostrils flare in disgust, and I absolutely love it. I continue pumping my cock as my orgasm rushes through me, erupting and decorating her pale skin. Some of my release lands on her hair, the side of her face, and lips. I am marking her and claiming her as my toy.

As the last bit of cum drips out of my semi-hard cock still gripped in my fist, it trickles on my fingers.

I smirk and kneel down on the cold cement. "Open your fucking mouth, or I will do it for you." She doesn't react, her face remaining unreadable. Squinting, I turn my head slightly. What will she do? Raising my fingers to her lips, she doesn't budge. Naughty toy, naughty Banksy.

With my free hand, I bring it up to her throat and squeeze it while at the same time using my body to force her onto her back as I straddle her.

"You had to make it difficult for yourself, Banksy. When will you learn?" I tsk, with my hand still gripping her neck.

I can see her lips form a hard line as my cum runs down the side of her face. Using my finger, I press it between her lips. Banks tries to fight it by keeping her lips tight, but I am stronger. Moving my hand from her neck to her jaw, I hold it tight so she can't squirm as I push my finger in, breaking past her lips to her clenched teeth, "I'll break them. Open them the fuck up."

She gives in.

Her eyes water in defeat. Her lip quivers under my touch.

As much as she is getting under our skin, this doesn't affect me. I don't care. She deserves every bit of this. It's justice.

"Take it. Swallow all of it."

Her tongue laps my finger, cleaning it off and swallowing, just as I instructed. I let her lick me a couple more times. I need her to feel as small as possible. My cock twitches, still out resting on her stomach. As I remove my fingers, her brows furrow and nostrils flare.

"Don't be stupid, Banksy." I warn her as I let go of her jaw. My fingerprints decorate her face in red. Fucking beautiful.

"You are disgusting," she spits at me.

"The difference between you and me is, I don't care what other people think of me and you do." I'm so close to her face, I can feel her breath on my skin.

"Leave it. Don't try to clean it off. I will see if you do and I will come back down for an encore performance, Banksy."

Getting up off of her, I tuck myself back in. When I look down at her, she is fighting with herself to keep showing any emotion in front of me.

Picking up my phone, I go to call Landon, but it switches to video call when answered. Loud music plays and Smiley waves at me. My brow hitches, color me curious.

The screen flips to show Landon and a bunny. Fuck, this is good. Bro has to be fucked up to have her on his lap. I kneel down next to Banksy and whisper, "Watch." She turns her head to look, but I keep her out of frame. I don't need anyone knowing about the toy we have locked in our basement.

Then, it happens.

Landon's lips lock with the bunny's, and my eyes shift to Banks. Hers are wide and her head shakes slightly. I'm not even sure she knows she is doing it. Then I hear Landon in the background, so I stand up again, positioning the phone just on me, and the call quickly ends. Fucking perfect.

Banks looks destroyed. Her slight glimmer of hope is completely washed away.

"You thought you were special, didn't you?" I begin taunting her. Her chest is heaving, eyes closed as she shakes her head.

"I know you're only doing this because if the scouts find out you're on probation with the team, academic probation, it puts a red flag on your file."

"Well fucking played, bitch. Who told you that? Landon? Did this big fucking mouth start talking once I hinted at his little secret?" My fists clench. I would be surprised if I didn't crush my phone at this point.

"If you would have done what you needed to fucking do, none of this would have happened. None of this would have been a fucking issue. Don't you understand? You fuck with us, we fuck with you. It's that simple, Banksy. Hopefully, this will teach you for next semester. Summer would be a long one down here, wouldn't it?" I threaten. The minute we get our grades we are fucking out of here to where ever I sign to, but she doesn't need to know that. Then realization washes over me. I just decided my future.

What is she doing to us?

CHAPTER 21

BANKS

It's been a few days since the night of the video call and Hudson cumming all over my face. I heard fireworks the other night which means New Year's Eve has come and gone. My body feels dirty. Not just from the dried cum in my hair and rubbed into my skin. Because contrary to what Hudson asked, I was not letting it just sit on me as it was until they let me out. My hair is greasy and while I would never admit it, if they offered me a shower in exchange for something, there is a good chance I would take it. I don't know what that says about me, but at this point I don't really care. Any shame I had is long gone. Nothing is beneath me considering my current circumstances.

Staring at the exposed ceiling, wires and wooden beams above me, I shake my head out of frustration. They have to let me out soon. The new school semester is going to start and people will wonder where I am if I don't show up. They have to let me out.

I have refused to cry since the first night. I keep reminding myself that I am strong, that I can make it through anything they throw at me. Only a couple more days. It has to be only a couple more days.

The guys have been more standoffish when they drop my food and water off. Apparently, the bait they gave me worked against them. The little joke or spat between them has escalated and I am being punished for it.

Speaking of the devils, I hear two sets of footsteps making their way down to me. The light has been on for hours, my concept of time is completely forgone.

"Hello, boys." The tone I greet them with is dull. It is usually them with their witty remarks when making their grand entrance, but this time, I beat them to it. Hudson smirks, I can tell he is impressed. His face shows everything, it is nearly impossible for him to hide anything. Landon remains unimpressed, his usual expression never changing. A phone rings, and Hudson puts his finger up, taking the call.

"Coach," is all he says when answering. My heart races. If I scream, he could help me. Or question why I hang out with students. Fuck. It's a fifty-fifty chance.

Landon's eyes zero in on me, silently daring me to do it and the temptation is strong. The consequences if I do, may not be worth it.

"Adams? Really? I mean yeah, of course. As long as he's good, Coach." Hudson responds. Lynx Adams left voluntarily, putting himself into rehab earlier this semester. He's Hudson's linemate and the team's left winger. The two of them together are unstoppable. I wonder if he is coming back. Landon is paying close attention to his brother, curious about what is being said on the other end of that phone. We don't have to wait long, Hudson hangs up shortly after.

Putting his phone away, he looks up at me while speaking to his brother. "Adams is coming back. But that's not why we are down here. Our time together is nearing its end and to commemorate it we are going to let you out of your collar and leash. Now, before you get excited, you are not leaving this house. We will be fucking on you the entire time, so don't even think about running. You know what could happen if you do." Hudson threatens. Regardless, a smile crosses my face.

"Shower? Does this mean I can shower?" He laughs at my question, "Sure Banksy, you can shower. But don't mistake this for us being nice, we can't have a mark around that delicate throat of yours from the collar. We can't have people asking questions, can we? It wouldn't look to good on us if word got out that we kidnap and torture staff, would it?"

I am getting out. Relief washes over me. Landon walks over with a key in hand, he still doesn't speak. I hurt him. I pitied him. I know exactly what I did and now he is closing himself completely off to me. A part of it hurts. I was only trying to care, to show compassion. Something I don't believe he has received much of. The lock clicks and he lifts it through the d-ring, dropping it onto the bed. Stepping back, he watches as I move my hands up and open the hinged metal from around me. Already I feel so much lighter as I remove it, placing it down on the bed. Cool air touches the skin on my neck for the first time in weeks. Rubbing the area, I am a bit sore from having the heavy object on me for so long. It feels strange no longer having it there.

"Get up." Landon barks, walking away. "It's time for your shower."

Like a puppy, I eagerly get up and follow both of them up the stairs, forgetting about grabbing my clothes as I am still in my bra and panties from the first night.

As we walk through the house, I can tell that for two guys it's really nice and clean. You can tell they take pride in their belongings. My bare feet pad against the hardwood as I follow the guys. I get hints of their musky colognes invading my nose, both are in gym shorts, with their strong, muscular hockey legs on display.

It's been a while since I have had sex. I'll admit it, years even. Toys and I are great friends, but something about these two men is doing things to my lady bits that shouldn't be happening. We enter a dark room, black walls, black bed, and windows covered by black curtains. It smells of Landon.

Woodsy and spicy with a hint of sweetness, something that matches his personality perfectly when I think about it.

Standing in the middle of his room, I bite on my thumb nervously as I take everything in.

"Don't just stand there, go with him," Landon barks at me as I look at him, confused. He nods his chin toward Hudson who is standing in the ensuite door frame.

Scurrying over, Hudson lets me pass and then follows behind. "Privacy, please?"

He laughs as he reaches into the glass shower, turning the tap on. Water begins coming out of the large shower head. Hudson closes the sliding glass door as it fills with steam and removes his sweater, exposing his muscular body. Then his thumbs go under his gym shorts and he pulls them down, he isn't wearing any boxers. His cock is semi-hard, is this man ever not horny?

"Eyes up here, Banksy."

His voice catches me off guard and my eyes meet his. He steps closer and reaches his arms around me, unlatching my bra then using the tips of his fingers to bring the straps down my arms. My body tingles in response, my pussy is throbbing. Watching as the cups of my bra lower, exposing my erect nipples, I can hear his breath hitch. As my bra drops to the ground, his thumbs go under the waist of my panties, and I don't stop him. He kneels before me as they slide off my body. His hand moves behind my knees, one at a time, forcing them to bend and step out of them, as they are currently bunched around my ankle. My breathing is heavy as his fingers trace along my leg. "You smell desperate." Hudson's voice rasps.

"Are you done touching me? I would like my shower now," I say carelessly, trying not to show how his touch arouses me.

"Banksy, I will never be done. You belong to us, remember that."

He stands up, opening the glass door and steps in. This motherfucker thinks he is showering with me.

"Is this really necessary?" I roll my eyes at him.

"Get the fuck in here. You wanted a shower, you are getting a shower. You will be watched the entire time you are in this house by either me or Landon."

"And when you let me go, how can you trust I won't tell anyone what you have done to me?" I challenge him, still standing naked in the cold bathroom.

Shaking his head, he rolls his eyes at me, "Get in the fucking shower before I change my mind." I give in immediately. I desperately need a shower, but will continue questioning him as I clean myself.

Closing the glass door behind me, I stand under the

warm spray of the water.

"Damn, I have missed this," I whisper into the water.

"And that's how I know you won't say anything. You value your freedom. This shower, not being chained again, not being jerked off on. Shall I continue to list them? Your job depends on it. What would the school think if they saw photos of us in the shower right now? My naked body against yours while you stand under the water. Your face filled with ecstasy." I can feel his hard cock against my back as he whispers, "My hands massaging your perky tiny tits as your back arches, your ass pushing into me as your head rests on my chest." My eyes close as he does exactly what he says. A moan escapes my mouth as his thumb and forefinger twist my nipple.

"Smile for the camera, Banksy."

My eyes shoot open. "What camera?"

He clears some of the steam off the glass, and Landon is standing on the other side of it with his camera phone in hand.

Motherfuckers!

Turning around, I push Hudson back. He stumbles before bracing himself on the shower wall with his hand.

"When will it stop? I fucked up, I didn't even know I fucked up. But according to the two of you, I did. And after hearing how, I get it. I do. I would be pissed too. What if you just applied yourself to fucking school instead of relying on someone to help you pay off your professors?"

It's Landon who speaks first, "But this way is much easier, and proving to be much more fun."

Hudson follows, letting out a sigh in frustration, "We have done this since freshman year. We accept we don't do books. We aren't smart in that way. Give me a fucking hockey stick and I am the best fucker out there. Give him pencils and paper, and he can draw the fuck out of anything. Give us a calculus exam, and we don't stand a fucking chance. So this is what we do. What we have done. Until you fucked us. Now wash your smelly fucking hair and desperate cunt and shut up. For once, just don't talk, please."

I will not cry. I will not let them get to me. Taking a deep breath, I reach around Hudson for the shampoo and lather it in my hair, not looking at either of them for the rest of the shower.

Landon left the bathroom and Hudson stayed. My body is wrapped in a thick warm towel with my wet hair hanging over my shoulders. "I need clothes please."

Hudson has put his clothes back on and heads out of the bathroom, only to return with a giant black tee and men's boxers. Placing them on the counter, he stands behind me and waits with his face hard and arms crossed. His eyes watch me in the mirror as I drop the towel and grab the boxers first, pulling them up my legs and resting them on my hips. They are way too big for me, but it's better than nothing.

I take in the mark he left on my ribs; it's healing nicely, but the scar will remain forever. Bringing my focus back to Hudson, I wink at him, showing him I know he is watching, but he isn't phased, so I throw the tee on next.

"You will be staying with Landon in his room. If you disobey him, he won't warn you before punishing you. He will just do it. Understood? Do not tempt him, he will bite and you will regret it." Hudson warns before walking out.

I just need to make it another day or two, then I am free, then I can go home.

CHAPTER 22

LANDON

Laying next to her as she sleeps is nearly intolerable.

As much as she pisses me and my brother off, I cannot deny there is something beneath all of this bullshit. I kissed her as a tactic. And it's fucking backfiring. Every minute I am not high on Venom or drowning in my art, it's her. She's all I see, all I fucking feel, and I hate it with every inch of my being.

She pitied me. How fucking dare she. I don't need her *poor Landon* eyes looking at me. I'm not weak. My brother and I are the strongest people I know. The shit we have gone through with our dad. No one else should have to.

The burnings, the constant watching, the taunting us

with something we desperately want just to take it away. Our mother. He will go to the grave with what happened to her. Bastard.

But is what we've done to Banks really any different? We tell each other it is. She stole, she narced, she fucked with the wrong people. Possibly jeopardizing Hudson's career. Jeopardizing my place in college. As long as I am here, I am not at home with that monster.

My mind is conflicted. It's too late to care or change what we have done to her. It's done. We did it. She won't make this mistake again. Mission accomplished.

The sound of my doorknob turning catches my attention, it's Hud. He walks in, not closing the door behind him. What the fuck is he up to?

Standing at the bottom of my bed, he holds something up. I can barely make it out, but it looks like rope. Looking over at Banks', her breathing is still shallow and even which means she is still asleep. She passed out quickly after the shower and eating, barely saying two words to us.

Hud throws some rope at me, and I know exactly what he is implying, I wrap it gently around her wrist closes to me, then secure it to my bed frame. The chick is out, doesn't even fidget. This is her first night in a proper bed and sheets in weeks, so it makes sense.

Looking up, Hudson has already secured her ankles and begins working on her other wrist. My cock twitches against my boxers. She is so accessible right now. I could do anything I fucking want to her and she wouldn't be able to stop me. To show her I don't need her fucking pity.

Hudson slowly rolls her long shirt up past her belly button and exposes her breasts. My finger reaches for her nipples, I have to know if she's hard. A chill washes over me as I trace her skin, once I reach her nipple, I circle it a couple times. Her body reacts to my touch, slightly moaning.

into it with each delicate move I make on her body. The art I could create on her would be endless. A nearly blank canvas, mine for the taking. Moving down her body, her stomach covered in goosebumps and her breath hitches. I stop and look at her, not moving while I patiently wait to see if her eyes open. Hudson is also focused on her, not making his next move either. Watching her chest rise and fall in the same rhythm as before, she is still out and I continue my descent to the loose fitting boxers blocking my access to her bare pussy.

Hudson wastes no time, gingerly shimmying them down her hips, then her thighs, leaving them resting at her knees. My finger acts on its own now, tracing mindless designs along her hip, then her pubic area. I am captivated by the tiny creature before me. No one has ever cared enough to have pity on me, on us. No one has ever been exposed to our lives like she has. Our dark and depraved side. And yet she still had compassion for us. Maybe it's something we will never understand, something that cannot be explained. Right now, I don't need any answers.

My finger pushes itself between her swollen lips, and she is fucking soaked. Inserting a finger into her pussy, I slowly rub her sensitive walls and use my palm to work her clit. Banks fidgets, but this time I don't check to see if she is awake, it wouldn't fucking matter. The sound of soft fabric dropping to the floor briefly catches my attention. It's Hudson. He is working his cock while watching me play with our pet, our toy.

Moving my finger faster, Banks' hips buck slightly against my hand. Her breathing has sped up and a small moan escapes her. Her pussy clamps around me and I pull my finger out, putting it between my lips and sucking her juices clean off me. She is heaven. My cock is rock hard pulling my own boxers down. I expose myself like my

163

brother and position myself between her legs. Gripping my cock, I line myself up to her entrance and thrust myself inside of her tight pussy. So tight it almost feels virginal. Screams echo in my ears. She's up, but I don't fucking care. Gripping her hips, I elevate her body, angling her as much as possible given the restraints we have her in and begin fucking her relentlessly. My hips buck rapidly as her pussy tightens even more around my cock.

Looking up with hooded eyes, Hudson has one hand over her mouth as he continues to work his length. She begins milking my cock, no longer fighting against the ropes that have her tied up. Banks gives into the moment, allowing her body to enjoy everything that is happening. As my cock rams inside of her a couple more times, my body tingles, and I throw my head back as my own release takes over. Ropes of my warm cum fill her, coating her walls and mixing with her own release.

"Such a good fucking girl. Letting me fill you up like this. Tied perfectly in my bed," I rasp.

Hudson lets out a groan of his own, my eyes move up her torso taking in her bouncing breasts as I continue my assault on her tight cunt. He decorates her body with his cum, making beautiful designs all along her skin. "Fucking take it. You know the rule, no cleaning it off," Hudson states as he continues to work himself all over her.

My movements slow down, and I place her hips back down on the bed while I am still inside of her. I don't fucking want to leave it. Hudson removes his hand from her mouth, but she doesn't scream or speak. She pants into the quiet room with the rest of us.

"I won't," she whispers, promising my brother. "I won't clean it off." Sliding out of her, I wish we had a light on so I could watch my cum drip out of her and onto my sheets. Taking my finger, I stick it inside of her, gathering up my release and bring it to her mouth. "Open." I instruct. She does, letting my finger pass through her lips and onto her tongue. She closes them around me and sucks, cleaning me off perfectly, moaning with each lap. I slowly pull it out of her, then lean down and kiss her forehead. "Our good girl," I praise her. I begin undoing the ropes, moving to the other side of her.

"Such a good little Banksy for us, aren't you?" I hear Hudson whisper to her. Then the sound of kissing follows.

I finish undoing one side of her and move to the other while they have their moment. Her body is free, but she doesn't move until she's done kissing my brother.

Hud pulls her boxers up, and before leaving the room, he whispers, "That includes your pussy, too. No cleaning. Understood?"

Banks swallows before whispering back, "Understood."

Hudson leaves the room, closing the door behind him. Neither of us speak for what feels like ages. Laying in silence, I can hear our rapid heartbeats slowing down. Eventually she breaks the quiet. "When my skin is healed, will you tattoo me there, like you do with yours?"

My eyes shut, this fucking girl. Shaking my head, the fucking nerve she has.

"Sorry. I shouldn't have asked," she says after I don't respond. Then she turns on her side with her back to me.

Fuck.

"Yes."

CHAPTER 23

HUDSON

It is return Banksy day.

After last night's fun, I am going to miss having her around and at our disposal.

The first night wasn't a good look for us. Kidnapping, drugging, and torturing with a skin grafter even if it was all necessary. She had to understand the magnitude of her fucking actions, unacceptable behavior, and stealing our money. Do I feel bad? Absolutely not. The light technique Landon thought of was a great psychological tool; she completely lost track of time and hope. You could see it in her eyes after the first couple of days.

Then, Landon became her hope just to crush her in a nice series of unplanned events and accidental video calls.

She was crushed. It was a beautiful thing to see.

And now, she is waking up more confused than when she got here. She is in Landon's room and he will have to deal with that pile of emotions.

Sitting on the couch, drinking my coffee, I wait for them to come downstairs so we can get this over with.

We have one final touch before releasing her into the world again, one final thank you for gifting us with team probation and bag skates every weekend.

Fucking bitch.

It's been fun fucking with her, but when I think about the shit we have to endure now because of her, it fills me with rage. Rage to the point of wanting to lock her in our basement until the end of time. But there is no point dwelling, one semester left. It is only one semester of ruined sleep and tired bodies.

Putting my coffee cup down on the table, I hop up and head to Landon's room. Would they hurry up already?

The lamp is on when I open the door. Landon hates light in his space unless it's his lamps by his drawing desk. Banks is smiling back at me when I look over to the bed where she is sitting fully clothed and looks to be showered. Landon must have collected her things from the basement.

"He is getting dressed." She looks at me timidly, and I nod, acknowledging her, but not saying anything.

Standing against the door frame, we wait for my brother. Finally, he comes out and takes one look at me already knowing what's next.

"Banks, we are doing this because we have to. You made us do this, it's almost fucking over I swear." Landon holds her face, convincing her that it will be ok. It won't. She will fucking hate this next part.

I walk over and her eyes find mine. Tears begin to well in hers and her face reddens. She is terrified.

Taking the syringe out of my pocket, I move quickly, jabbing it into her neck and pushing down until everything in it is gone.

Venom.

"No, no, no," she whimpers, holding onto Landon's biceps. Her pupils dilate almost immediately. This chick is going to be seeing shit for hours. This was our only choice, we don't need her remembering how to get to our house.

Tears trail down her cheeks. I want to feel bad, but I don't. This was always the game plan.

"Keep your eyes open and relax, breathe in and out Banks. Stay calm, it won't be as bad as long as you just relax," Landon tries to coax her down from her anxiety.

She nods, trying to regulate her breathing, then whispers. "You kissed her and it made me so mad. You kissed her on purpose and had him show me on purpose." Landon looks at her confused.

"Now is not the time for this conversation, Banks. It's time to go home." I cut in.

I provide a round trip service, she came into the house over my shoulder and she will be leaving it the same way. Nudging Landon, he moves out of the way reluctantly. I grab Banksy and toss her over, and slap her ass for good measure.

"No, you're making it spin. Please make it stop." I roll my eyes at her, this girl cannot handle drugs, fuck.

Landon grabs the keys to the Rover, and we head out.

Banks is laying in the backseat when we pull up to

her apartment. It's early enough in the morning that no one should see us. And if they do, we are just helping our advisor out with something.

Getting out of the car, I open the back door. It's closest to her place so less people can sneak a peek if they happen to be lurking. We both help Banks get out of the car. Her eyes are still closed, and she has been practicing her breathing the entire fucking ride here, no idea if it's working, but she hasn't been complaining as much. I wrap my arm around her neck casually, so she can lean on me as we walk. Landon walks slightly ahead of us, unlocking her door, then shouts, "Ms. Lewis, which light did you need help with in here?"

This kid is smart. She doesn't reply, so I do for her, "It was her living room one, dumbass. She just told you." He rolls his eyes at me and heads inside, we follow behind, closing the door. We get inside and he takes her from me. Her place is small, with an open living room and kitchen with a hallway that has two rooms off it.

"We are going to put you to bed. I put my number in your phone if you need anything, but you should be fine. It will wear off in a couple of hours and you will be fine. Just enjoy the fucking ride, Banks. See the fucking stars floating in front of you, got it?" Landon tells her as we make it into her room. It is pretty bare, only a bed, dresser, and a chair in the corner. I lift the blankets up on her bed as he sits her down on the edge, kneeling down to take her shoes off, then grabbing her ankles and rotating her to lay down. She looks up at us through her long lashes, her green eyes unable to focus.

"Don't get up. Just ride this shit out. It's going to be fine. Landon will bring you some water in case you get thirsty, but just lay here and breathe. Remember what I said, breathe in and out, ok?" I hear Landon's footsteps

170

walking out behind me. My hand cups her cheek as she nods against it, acknowledging what I am saying.

"Good job, Banksy."

Landon comes back in with a glass of water, placing it on her nightstand.

"You call us and only us if you need anything, understood? You will be ok, give it a couple hours and you will be fine." Landon reassures her. I only gave her half the dosage we did the night we took her, so it's not nearly as intense of a trip this time around. He leans over, kissing her forehead before he heads out of her room.

As we leave her apartment, I yell back inside, "See you at practice, Ms. Lewis." Playing off the rest of our charade as if nothing has happened. Just as we close the door behind us, my phone vibrates in my pocket. It's Coach. Picking it up as we walk to the Rover. "Coach, miss me already?"

"Fuck's sake, Cooper, it's way too early for your shit. Adams is coming in tomorrow, which means I have to rework the lines. So the guys I have to move will also be here. Which means you have to fucking cuddle them after I tell them of the line changes or whatever the fuck it is you do to make them feel better. Suck their cocks, I don't know and I don't care, Cooper. Just fucking be here early. Adams will bag skates and workout with you guys. I have no fucking clue what shape he is coming back to us in. Understood?" Coach Taylor shouts at me through the phone.

Landon is snickering next to me. "Sorry, Coach, but I think I misheard you. You want me to cuddle the guys, then suck their dicks to make them feel better after you tell them about the line changes tomorrow? On Sunday? The day of the lord and you would like me to honor him by doing that?"

"Cooper, you motherfucker. I said it is too early for

your shit, didn't I? Be at the rink by six am. Bring your brother, we are starting early tomorrow. How is that for celebrating the lord's day?" Then he hangs up the phone.

Landon and I both burst out laughing hysterically. Coach was on one today. Every so often he gets riled up, and this is one of those times. With line changes mid-season while we are on a winning streak. Guy has to be freaking out. I'm not worried, we are an adaptable team. Change challenges us and only makes us stronger. Plus, getting Lynx back is a fucking relief. He is my right hand on the ice, and I have fucking missed him this season. Don't get me wrong, Smitty has been awesome, but Lynx and I have played together for years. We know each other's next move before we even do it. You can't beat that level of on-ice chemistry.

"Fuck bro, lets get out of here." I'm still laughing as Landon shakes his head, smirking while putting the Rover into gear and takes off.

What a fucking morning this has been.

CHAPTER 24

BANKS

Coach sent a text late the other night letting me know about Lynx Adams coming back to the team. I'll need to set up a meeting with him, review his classes, and make a game plan to keep him on track. He also warned me about some line changes, so come Monday, a few guys could be in bad moods and to not take it personally. I appreciated the heads up.

I'm still recovering from the shit the guys injected me with yesterday. I barely slept. Even when my eyes were closed, vivid images would wash over me. It felt like if I reached out, I could touch the stars. They were blue and pink and the moon was bright yellow. All of it surrounding me as I lay in bed.

Anytime I moved my head, they would move too, following me like I was their center. I should have felt honored having an entire universe focused on me, but in reality, it only made me feel dizzy and nauseous.

I hated it so much.

I felt like I was on the verge of crying, but I couldn't, it wouldn't let me. And my heart left my chest, floating in front of me, dark blue and red, beating rapidly. My hands tried to move it back inside of me, but it wouldn't go back. By the time the trip ended, it was well into the night. I was exhausted but still afraid to close my eyes.

Coach is the only person I've heard from since getting my phone back. A part of me was hopeful the guys would check in, make sure I was alive.

I'm only kidding myself with those thoughts, that will never happen. Delusional as the drugs. That's me.

But as my mind wanders, I cannot help but think back on these past couple of weeks. Underneath all the ego, the mystery, and athletics, they are just two men who deserve the same love, compassion and protection from evil that the rest of us have. But what does one do when they are evil, and you crave more and more of it? When you don't want protection from their evil, from them?

Standing up out of frustration, with myself and this entire fucking mess, I go to the kitchen and open my junk drawer. It's where I put the money after I found it under my door that morning. They even divided it up perfectly for me. No math needed, all I had to do was hand it off to their professors.

Easy, right?

Not for me because here it sits in my home. Squeezing my eyes shut, I place my head down on the counter. I had no idea. If I had, I would have done it, maybe? The me of two weeks ago wouldn't have. Who am I kidding? But I would have given their money back to them, told them they were out of their ever loving minds if they thought I would be their mule. Current me might have done it. Knowing what I know now, there is a strong possibility I would have helped those boys. It's why I'm their advisor, to help them, to get them to graduation and walk across that stage collecting their degrees. To be able to play the sport they love and to fucking succeed. That is my job.

I have to do it when midterms come. Again for finals. May as well get used to the idea of it now.

I should be so mad right now. Should be enraged. I should be going to the police and reporting these sick and depraved bastards. They should be getting their daddy to pay for the best attorney money can buy to keep them out of jail.

The school and hockey association should be notified. Show them my scars, the brandings they placed on my body. Lifting my head up, I take a deep breath and open my eyes. I should be really fucking pissed, but... I'm not.

This person, this strange fucking person I have become, isn't mad. She sees past their tough exterior. She sees all their broken pieces that lead them to the place they are now.

Does this make me broken too?

I slam the drawer closed. It's settled.

Fuck the moral high ground.

Monday morning has come and gone. I've been in my office the entire time, pulling Lynx's grades, class schedule, and reading the notes on his file. All his previous professors say he was always quiet in class, keeping to himself and maintained decent grades.

The grades piece surprises me.

Addiction, combined with playing hockey, and staying on top of school isn't the norm. He is Hudson's winger, his go-to person. With my knowledge of addiction, it takes over your entire life, so the fact that he managed to stick with it all until it ultimately became too much is impressive. He went into rehab voluntarily too. He seems like a genuinely good kid that just got caught up in some bad shit.

It also notes that he is close with Raiden King, one of our defenseman, on the same line as Landon. Put those two together on ice, and watch out. It's really an impressive showing.

He may just need some meetings at the beginning to get him used to being back, the routine and schedule. Then maybe move it to bi-weekly check-ins if everything seems like it is on track.

The guys haven't popped in at all. Every so often, I hear someone walking by and I look up, wondering if it's them. Coach checked in earlier; his mood seemed different. Maybe he had a rough holiday on top of the line changes. I lied about mine, obviously.

What was I going to say? *Oh boy, I had the best time ever. I was forced to spend it in a cold basement and was practically naked all break. Let me tell you, the bed was a five-star stay. The best part was when I had to shit in a bucket with dried cum on my body. Highly recommend staying at the Cooper boys' house the next chance you get.*

Instead, I told him it was quiet, hung out at home, and relaxed. It was anything but that. If he only knew what lays beneath my sweater.

It's getting cold in Groveton, colder than it was in December. Perfect for hockey season.

Getting up and deciding to escape the four walls I have barricaded myself in most of the day, I'm not paying attention when I bump into a strong body.

"Watch where you're going." His voice is harsh and his familiar scent washes over me. I step back while continuing to look down at my feet. "Sorry, that was my fault. I wasn't paying attention."

His breath hits the side of my face, and Landon whispers in my ear, "Look at me when you speak. Understood?"

"I understand." I whisper with a nod and look up at him.

"You miss us?"

Chills roll down my spine, my face remains neutral, not giving anything away. "No," I shrug while keeping eye contact.

"Liar."

My breath hitches at his accusation, but I don't respond.

"You loved it. You need it. You can't help yourself from wondering if it will ever happen again." My head shakes slightly in response, but he continues, "I can smell your desperate pussy from here, Banks. Stop. Lying."

His last words bite. He meant them to sting.

Still keeping eye contact, I stand there, challenging him with my silence. His eyes squint as his head turns slightly. The stand-off continues until we hear loud footsteps coming toward us. His eyebrows raise.

"Until we meet again, Ms. Lewis. Thank you for all that you have done for me and my brother," he winks as he walks away.

Letting out a sigh of relief once the owner of the loud footsteps turns the corner. "Cooper, get changed and hit the gym. No options. Only workouts," Coach Taylor shouts. Landon nods in response and continues to the locker room. That is the Landon I know—or knew. The quiet, observant, and calculated one. Now I know another side to him, with more still to peel off, layer by layer. Just like they did to me.

CHAPTER 25

HUDSON

It's game night, baby. Fucking love this sport.

Adrenaline is coursing through my veins as I wrap my stick with tape. Tonight we play Texas State, bunch of pussies. Their delicate state bodies can't even handle checks without crying to the refs. Just wait fuckers, we will really give you something to cry about if you try this shit again.

I chuckle to myself at the thought of Landon and Raiden throwing gloves with them. I, Hudson Cooper, the ever-so-morally-stable captain, would try and stop the madness, naturally. But those guys, our defensive duo, you can't get between them, their fist and someone's face. So this morally high ground captain might just have to let it happen, I suppose.

"Bro, what's so funny?" Landon questions.

"Ah, brother. I am just thinking about the pussy. Tonight is going to be a great game," he stares back at me confused, unsure on how to respond, so he doesn't. Landon nods and goes back to taping his own stick.

Before returning my focus back on getting ready, Lynx walks into the locker area. His dark brows are furrowed, and his California bleach blond hair hangs over his forehead, he looks stressed. Motherfucker.

"Adams! Do not fuck this game up tonight with your nerves. You know how to play hockey. The minute your skate hits the ice for warm up, you will fucking judge yourself for being so in your head. It's like riding a bike. You can't fuck that up and you won't fuck this up. Got it?" I am also really good at motivational speaking.

Lynx stands, absorbing my words and his head begins to nod. "Yeah, I know. First game back nerves and I don't want to fuck up the team's winning streak. A lot of changes were made so I could come back. It's a lot, but it's fine. You're right, man."

I roll my eyes, of course I am. "You're my guy, you know my moves before I make them. There is nothing to worry about. Just let the magic fucking happen." I stand up, and walk over to him, putting my arm around his shoulder. "Tell your nerves they are no longer needed here. We are fine. You are fine and let's go play some old-fashioned puck." A few of the guys cheer at my last statement. We fucking love this game.

Lynx pushes me playfully away as he mutters to himself, now he's smiling. Fucking right.

Sitting back in my locker, I look up at the clock. We don't have much time before warm-up to get ready. I finish wrapping my stick and put my gear on, popping my helmet on last.

"Alright boys, let's fucking go." I shout into the room, and I head out to the hallway leading to the ice.

Back in the dressing room after warm-ups, Lynx had nothing to worry about. The guy stepped on the ice and immediately got his confidence back. Coach is standing by his whiteboard shouting plays at us and the first period game plan. I know the drill, forecheck, backcheck, paycheck. The paycheck will come when I sign to the pros. I can smell it, almost taste it. A few more months. We aren't allowed agents in college, but there's a guy I know and we talk regularly about my future. I still haven't told him that I'm going to see if we can line up a team and sign out of college. It's crazy to think that snatching Banks helped make such a massive life decision.

"Cooper, are you paying attention to me?" Coach Taylor shouts. Motherfucker.

"Yes, sir. We got this. Check Hard. Play Hard. Fuck Hard." The guys join in and shout fuck hard with me.

"You little shits, I said enough of that goddamn chant."

Yeah, not going to happen. We have been doing this all season. It's part of the pregame ritual now. Lynx is laughing, he hasn't heard this one yet.

Smiley stands up first. "Alright boys, let's get 'er done!" Others cheer while standing up, fist bumping each other with our gloves, and head out to the ice.

The first period was a breeze, we kept the pussies out of our zone and put the pressure on them the entire period. It showed in the second. They were determined at the start. Forcing us back into our own zone to defend Barlowe, but their determination slowly waned. They are getting tired. Amateurs.

There's ten minutes left in the third period. It's a scoreless game. Frustrating as fuck. I'm on the bench waiting for my shift. My legs are bouncing from the anticipation and wanting to keep them warm and moving. The place is packed and the crowd boos when the linesman's arm goes up.

Motherfucker, he caught the offside. Just barely too. Play stops, forcing a faceoff outside their zone.

My eyes hone in on the puck, it's slow motion, watching the black puck drop to the ice, and two sticks battle for control, with State winning it. Our guys bust their asses to keep it out of our net. My heart is racing as the guys jump over the boards and our line heads out.

My legs push my body to get to the puck as fast as possible to take back control of this game. This is home. The rink, the fans, this game. My stick connects with the puck. I need to get it out of our zone. I make it to center ice before some pussy decides to try and stop me with their stick. Whistle blows, the play stops, a two minute hooking penalty against State is called. It's time for a power play.

I am on the power play special teams, so are Lynx, Landon, Raiden and Smitty.

I take the face off, winning it, of course. It's five on four and we are in their motherfucking zone. Now is the time.

Smitty has the puck as we get into formation. State scrambles to protect their net as we pass the puck around, waiting for the right moment. Smitty whistles as a distraction, making them think the puck is going to him. I pass it to Lynx, who takes the opportunity and shoots. The ring of the puck off the side of the metal goal post make my eyes widen with anticipation.

Go in, please go in.

The entire rink collectively gasps. Then goes silent.

It goes in.

He did it. Lynx is back. We rush at him, hugging him in celebration. Patting his helmet I look at him in the eyes, "Play hard. Check hard. Fuck hard." He laughs, his eyes almost teary with pride. He is fucking back.

Skating back to center ice, I look up at the crowd.

Same spot every game.

Black hair is down and over her shoulders. She has our team hoodie on and leggings. Her hands are still clapping together with a smile on her face that reaches her beautiful green eyes.

She catches me looking at her, and it takes her back.

I wink.

She bites her lip and winks back.

I look over at my brother, he sees her too, acknowledging her with a slight nod.

A smirk forms on my face. Such a good Banksy.

The game finishes. We won, 1-0. Back in the locker room, we are taking our gear off and getting ready for the showers.

But before that, we have a surprise for Lynx. Smiley is over in his locker giggling like a goddamn school girl. He knows exactly what's coming.

Player of the game.

Barlowe got it before break. It's his turn to pass it on. Picking our only goal scorer of the night, Lynx.

"Buddy, we are excited to have you back with us. There's not a piece of rust on your old bones, you fit back in like you never left." The guys laugh at the rusty bones comment as Barlowe continues, "Not only do I gift you player of the game, but I give you our player of the game belt."

We whistle, lighting up the room. Barlowe passes the cheap wrestling championship belt to Lynx, who is smiling ear to ear. He examines the emblem on the front, it says 'The People's Champ' which is a famous wrestler's saying. Then, in the middle, is that motherfucker's face: Lynx Adams, with his eyebrow raised, looking tough as fuck. He busts out laughing.

We did some photoshop, added his features to the wrestler's face once we heard he was back.

"I look so fucking stupid on this thing," he chuckles, still examining it, "But yeah, thank you guys for having me back and it felt amazing being back out there."

"Of course, man, always. Now lets shit, shower and shave boys and hit up Graves to celebrate."

"Don't party too hard tonight. You need to be back here, 9am tomorrow!" Coach announces then leaves the room.

Drug test.

CHAPTER 26

LANDON

Tonight we are hitting up the off campus bar called Graves. This place is a fucking dive with old wooden stools lining the bar, a burgundy fabric covers the tops and inside of the booths against the walls. Tables have mismatched chairs around them as decent music plays.

The lighting is dim, with Groveton sports paraphernalia displayed proudly everywhere. This shit goes back decades. There are signed jerseys from players who made it big decorating the walls. This place is known for its mediocre cheap beer, perfect for college students, disgusting to the likes of my brother and me. With the drug test tomorrow, we had to stay away from the frats, too easy to snort a line of coke or take a hit off a joint, then we'd get burnt on the drug test. I'm sure some guys pay for clean piss. I have in the past, but since Venom was introduced there has been no need for it. If I really need to escape before a test, that's my go to, undetectable. The Noxious Boys really knew what they were doing making that shit. But some guys on the team are too easily tempted, so tonight, we celebrate at Graves.

Our team claims the booths against the wall. Me and a couple guys volunteer to get glasses and pitchers. A few of the bunnies followed us here, sitting at the tables just off to the side, looking desperate for a fuck. As I wait for the bartender to fill my order I watch them, they are pointing to a few fourth line guys, probably discussing who they are going to try to fuck tonight. They know most of us won't touch them with a ten-foot pole, nevermind our cocks.

A hand on my shoulder startles me, turning my head it's a tiny blonde thing, looking up at my stone cold face with doe eyes. "Sorry, I was trying to squeeze in so I could order a drink," she says innocently. I believe her. My eyebrows lift, acknowledging her as I turn my body so she can fit in.

"Thank you," she bites her lip. She isn't done, fucking great. "I'm Courtney."

Rolling my eyes, "I don't care what your name is." Her face scowls at my response.

"Hey man, here's your pitcher. On the house, congrats on the win tonight," the bartender says. I nod in gratitude and leave 'Courtney' alone.

The place is filling up. Word has gotten out the team is celebrating here, and loads of students are starting to stumble in from the rink.

I didn't see Banks after the game. Sometimes she will come in after a win, this time she didn't. We both saw her cheering from the stands. That girl has done something to my head.

The moment we scored, I celebrated with my brothers, my team. Then I had to see her. She was just as excited as we were over the goal. Hudson did the same. She's caught us both, just like we caught her.

Approaching my booth, I place the beer and glasses down, the boys cheer and start pouring. Sliding in next to Raiden, he elbows me, leaning down, "Something on your mind?" The guy can be a dick. He's an absolute beast of a player, but he is great at reading people. It's what makes him a great hockey player.

Shaking my head, "No man, I spaced out for a minute, I guess. I'm good." He nods, accepting my response and doesn't push me. He knows I'm bullshitting, but respects that I don't want to talk about it.

Hudson lifts his glass, "Alright boys, listen up," all the booths filled with our guys stop and focus on Hud, the bar goes quiet as others watch and listen.

"Adams...Lynx. We couldn't be happier to have you back and you showed us tonight how much you are meant to be here, with us, on this team, playing the sport we fucking love. You didn't fuck up and we are still on our way to the playoffs, baby! To Lynx, for scoring in his first game back and for not fucking up!" Lifting up our glasses, we all cheer at my brother's speech. He has a way with words.

Adams is embarrassed by the attention, but the guy played hard tonight, he deserves this.

A few hours pass into the night, it's well past one in the morning, and a few guys have left already while the rest of us are still here drinking.

My mind wanders back to Banks, she better be sleeping. Looking around the bar, I see the blonde is still here at a table with a few other chicks I have never seen. My eyes go to the table full of bunnies next. One was lucky enough and snagged a guy, the others look miserable. They know who's left isn't interested.

I don't know how Hudson does it. He's fucked a couple random chicks since Banks, coming home smelling and looking like sex. How is he doing it? So easily forgetting what happened in the basement and my room.

Standing up from the booth, I walk over to the blonde, and tilt my head toward the ladies room. She gets up to follow me.

Walking into the bathroom, I kick open the three stall doors to make sure no one else is in here. Once the blonde is in I lock the main door behind her.

"Turn around, pull your pants down, and hold onto the sink. This is going to be hard and fast." She nods and does what I said.

I follow suit, taking my cock out and wrapping it with a condom, lining it up with her soaked entrance, I slam myself into her. Blondie moans, it echoes on the tile walls as I continue to pound into her cunt. My dick is barely hard as I watch her in the mirror. Closing my eyes, I try to picture anything to make this more enjoyable. My brain shows me Banks, in my bed when I took her for the first time. My hips continue to buck against the blonde, she whimpers, "Why are your eyes closed?" Great, her feelings are hurt. Fucking chicks.

I open my eyes again and the image of Banks leaves me, the rush in my cock going with it. This needs to end, fast.

Grabbing onto her hips, I thrust myself viciously into her until I feel her walls clamp around me. She milks my cock as her own orgasm hits, soaking my cock. Her movements slow down, as do mine. My heart is racing as I pant slightly, letting a grunt escape from between my lips. Letting go of her, I pull out, she's dripping from her own release. I tie my condom up and toss it in the trash as I tuck myself back in. She rakes her fingers through her hair, her face is glowing and is decorated with a smile.

"That was fucking amazing."

My face remains expressionless. "Good, now go." She is taken aback by my bluntness, but scurries out after unlocking the door.

Looking at the mirror, I turn the tap on and splash my face with cold water. Looking back up as it drips off my face, I judge myself slightly. It didn't even work. The minute I closed my eyes, it was her. It is always her, invading my thoughts, my dreams and my art.

Fuck.

Oh, and that performance just now? That was me faking an orgasm for the very first time.

CHAPTER 27

BANKS

The guys were all drug tested this past weekend. I just got the results back, along with the coaching staff.

They all passed. Not a hint of drugs in anyone's system.

Don't get me wrong, I am ecstatic, but it's not like these guys. I know they party, and they go big. But who am I to question a good thing? The team is still intact. The guys are still happy. I am not going to ruin it with my curiosity.

I scroll through a few more emails from the professors that contain updates on assignments and quizzes, and add them to my calendar. Each player has their own color code, so I can keep track of it all and follow up with them on it. This is what keeps me organized or I would be absolutely all over the place.

A new email pops up from the coach replying to the drug test results, a simple thank you, acknowledging he got them. Seconds later, a knock on my open door catches my attention, it's Coach Taylor. That was quick, he must have replied from his phone.

"Hey Coach, I saw all the guys passed. That's great news for the team." His face doesn't give away what he's thinking.

He clears his throat. "How are the Coopers doing? I know we are only two weeks into the new semester, but I can't have them fucking up midterms. We need them for playoffs, Banks."

The last time I had any interaction with them was at the game, when they both looked at me after the goal by Lynx.

"Uh, yeah, no, everything looks good for the boys. A paper due next week for Hudson and an art project for Landon before midterms. I will check in with them later this week to make sure everything is on track. Both are attending their classes. No news is good news, for now." Reassured, he nods, absorbing what I've told him.

"Good, good. Banks..." he steps further into my office. "You're doing a great job here. You are about the team. It doesn't go unnoticed. Thank you."

I'm taken aback, not at all expecting this from Coach Taylor. "Wow, thank you. That means a lot. I do, I just want these guys to succeed no matter where they go from here. I appreciate you saying that, Coach."

"Just call it like I see it. You're a perfect fit for us," he turns around to head out, but stops just before stepping through the frame. Looking back at me, he winks then takes his leave. My body freezes, what in the hell was that for?

It's finally the end of the day, the skies are dark and the air is cold as I walk through campus to my car.

It almost feels like a storm is coming, and that's unusual for January in Groveton, so I hope I am wrong.

My short legs move as fast as they can to get back into warmth. The wind blows through my hair, chilling my ears. I can barely feel my face.

My car is in sight and it looks like someone has put a flier on my windshield. So annoying and a waste of their money, I never read them and I doubt many do. As I reach my car, I grab it and get in. I go to throw it in my backseat, but notice a white piece of paper sticking out of it. It doesn't match the rest of the flier coloring, so I'm curious.

Banksy,

We are always watching. Not a word to anyone. You know the consequences. How are your grafts healing?

That's it. I flip it over to double check that I'm not missing anything, but it's blank.

This is the first time I have heard from Hudson since they dropped me off. I know it's him because of his pet name for me, *Banksy.* Landon doesn't call me that.

I hold the note close against my chest, and lean back against the headrest. A sick part of me misses them. The depraved degradation, the blunt and raw emotion that Hudson would give me, the silent gentleness mixed in with the psychological aggression that Landon has.

I close my eyes, and memories of it all flash before me. What they did was horrible. Why they did it is even worse.

The threat of it happening again makes me desperate for their attention. As much as we despised each other toward the end, something changed. Call it crazy, call it Stockholm syndrome, or just plain stupidity. Something clicked on that last day, that moment in bed when we all came together. We wanted to. We needed to. And it was perfect.

Opening my eyes, I look out the windshield, but no one is around. Keeping the note close to my chest, I slide my other hand down the front of my navy blue leggings, my oversized winter coat hides what I am doing, should someone walk up or past me.

My panties are soaked. I use my thumb to play with my clit and my eyes grow heavy, picturing their big, thick veiny cocks. Hudson loved jerking off on me. He would grip it harder with each stroke, playing with his head and precum. Landon pushed his into me without mercy. My first fuck in years and it was with him. Ramming into my pussy, squeezing my petite frame with his hands, so possessively that I had his prints on my body for days following.

I insert two fingers into my cunt, finding the sweet spot, working it alongside my clit. My head falls back again against my headrest, my breathing picks up and my chest moves rapidly the faster I go.

A moan escapes me, as I continue to picture the guys with me, cumming inside and on me. My walls clamp around my two fingers as I continue to rub my g-spot. My legs tingle in anticipation.

Fuck yes, this feels so good.

My orgasm erupts on my fingers, my walls clamping around my fingers as my thumb frantically works my clit through it. Tingles run from my toes to my pussy. My body feels electrified. I buck my hips as I continue to work myself through my release.

Once it starts to subside, I remove my fingers, and an aftershock comes over me, my pussy clenches as it continues to spasm. Slowly, I remove my hand from my leggings, my fingers glisten and my face feels flushed. My breathing is heavy as I realize I have nothing to clean myself with.

Sticking my fingers in my mouth, I suck my cum off. My tongue lapping them, getting every last salty drop. As I withdraw them, I wipe the remaining saliva on my pants. Focusing back to outside, it's gotten darker out. The sun sets fast and early in the winter. No chance anyone saw my performance here in the school parking lot.

Before I can start my car, my phone buzzes on my passenger seat. I pick it up, it's from an unknown number,

Good Girl, Banksy.

CHAPTER 28

LANDON

I'm at my desk working on my midterm project. The table light is the only thing brightening my space as I've kept my curtains closed. This piece has to represent something that haunts us when we sleep at night and frightens us during the day. It's like someone told them this is exactly what is happening to me right now and made it into a project.

My professor claims confronting it is a therapeutic technique, not only an art assignment. It has many layers, and she wants to see us dig deep inside ourselves and expose each layer in our work.

My charcoal pencil works vigorously on the page, after a few lines I drop it and smudge some of it with my fingers, turning it into shading. I am barely thinking with the piece, allowing my hands and pencil to take over.

The art is naturally flowing out of me. Not critically analyzing anything in it. If a line isn't perfect, then that's how it should be. If the professor wants us to display our souls on paper, our nightmares and fears, then that is exactly what she will get from me. I've spent hours on this already, only half way done with a week to go. I'm not worried. When it's done, I'll know. My pencil will drop and my hands will fall back. And that is when I'll know.

The door slams, catching my attention. Looking at my phone, it's time for a break anyway, I have been at this desk for hours. Another door slams inside the house, but it sounds like it's coming from downstairs. What the fuck?

Pushing my chair back, I stand up, and brush my hands off on my pants, and go downstairs to look around.

Through the window I can see Hudson's car, so he is home. In the kitchen, there's still no sign of my brother. As I turn to leave, a light under the basement door catches my attention. Opening the door, I head down the stairs, I haven't been back down since she left.

As I reach the bottom, I see Hudson sitting on the edge of the mattress with his elbows on his knees, head in his hands.

"Dude, what's going on?" I question him. He doesn't respond, so I go sit next to him. What is happening with my brother?

We sit in silence in this dingy, cold basement. The chain is still attached to the floor, the sheet and pillow are still on the bed. The bucket is gone. We dumped that into the trash immediately after getting home from her place.

"How do you do it?" Hudson breaks the silence, still resting his head in his hands.

Confused by his question, "What do you mean, do

what?"

He sighs. "The only way I can cum anymore is if I picture myself coming all over her tits."

Ah, Banks.

Before I can answer, he continues, "Am I like dad? Getting off on the torture?" His voice is full of emotion. How long has he been beating himself up for this and not talking about it?

"You and me are nothing like father. I mean nothing. She's in my head too, man. Knowing you were hooking up with chicks after, I was so jealous. Wondering how the fuck can you move on so quickly, why can't I?" He looks up at me, shocked by my confession that so closely matches his own.

"I haven't fucked anyone since that chick you tossed off my cock. Blowjobs only. My eyes have to be closed though and coming on Banksy's tits is on repeat in my head. It's the only way it works."

I laugh at that, it's nice hearing I'm not the only one fucked. "Dude, I tried to fuck a chick in the bathroom the first game back, at Graves. You know I told you about the blonde. What I left out was, she demanded I look at her and I couldn't do it. I couldn't finish."

Before I can finish the sentence, Hudson laughs, "Dude, you faked it?"

"Yeah, I fucking faked it. Never in my life did I think those words would come out of my mouth."

We both get lost in our thoughts again. Sitting in silence, with our breathing the only noise coming from either of us.

I rub my face with both my hands, conflicted on what we do next.

"I left a note on her car last month, letting her know we were still watching. After she read it, she finger fucked herself in her car while holding it close to her chest. I watched, I was in the fucking trees on campus waiting for her maybe only five minutes to make sure she got it. And I watched her lick her fingers after smiling. Then I texted her, I got her number from your phone."

I cut him off, "What? How did you get in my phone?"

"We are twins, dumbass. Same eyes." This motherfucker, when else has he done this?

"I know what you're thinking. That was the first time I tried it and I didn't know it would even work. But back to what I was saying, after I watched her, I sent a text saying *good girl.* It was the hottest thing I have ever seen."

"So what do you suggest we do now?" He asks, tortured by feelings neither of us have felt before.

"We aren't him. Father gets off on hurting us, he thrives on our fear. We liked fucking with Banksy and toward the end she liked it too. Let's get through midterms, make sure she does what she's fucking supposed to and figure shit out when we get back after Spring Break. We both have a meeting with her about our classes before then, and we will remind her of her job and see what happens from there."

If she fucks us again, it's done. *She's* done. Banks will never see daylight again after the semester ends. You don't fuck us twice and get away with it. If she does what we need her to do, what she promised to fucking do, it makes shit a whole lot more complicated. We are twenty-one year old men who are battling our emotions and it's making us very uncomfortable. It's consuming our lives and taking over our minds. There is no more escaping it. It's time to face it head on.

Standing up, I grab my brother's shoulder and squeeze it. He looks up at me and nods.

"We will figure this out. One way or another, we will.

I promise, Hud." I am the more emotional one, internally, never showing much on my exterior. He is putting his faith in me now and I can't let him down.

As I walk up the stairs, Hud shouts, "As much as I want to fuck her, I want to her hurt more, man. She got off on that shit too. I know it."

Yeah, so do I.

"Go to sleep man, we have bag skates in the morning." Reminding him of our physical torture on the ice is all I can give him right now, because it's the only answer I have.

CHAPTER 29

BANKS

Time has been a blur. It's already the end of February, midterms are approaching and so is spring break. The guys are in the playoffs, so after the break they are full steam ahead in that round robin.

I have a meeting with the twins today. I've held it off as long as possible. We've been cordial in the locker room if we run into each other, but not much contact has been made since I got the '*good girl*' text and note.

"Ah, Ms. Lewis. Long time no see," Hudson walks into my office first. He winks when I look up and takes a seat in the chair across the desk from me. Landon follows, "Ms. Lewis," and closes the door.

"Hey guys, so," before I can finish, Hudson brings his chair forward, getting closer to the desk and me.

"You will use the cash you already have and pay the professors like they should have been paid at finals. We are paying them that money for midterms and we will give you another fifteen grand at finals. We normally do not pay at midterms, because who fucking cares about them? But you will not fuck up our final semester for us. We need to graduate and get the fuck out of here. Understood?" His voice is stern as his nostrils flare. His eyes laser focused on mine. No doubt he senses my fear.

"How? Do they even know it's coming? That it is from you guys?"

Hudson laughs at my question, "Of course they know it's coming. The professors from last semester are pissed they didn't get shit. So your cut goes to them. It's your job to fix this, you are no longer getting paid for it."

The money would have been nice, but it doesn't matter. I'll give it away to whoever they tell me to if it means I don't get locked up again. My body is shaking, "I understand. I'll do it."

He slaps the top of the desk with his hand, the sound startles me causing me to jump in my chair.

"Good girl, Banksy," he says smirking.

"So what, we kill time now. Make it seem like we are talking about how we are such bad boys and need to improve our grades? I'd rather do bag skates or mandatory workouts." Landon says casually, sitting back in his chair with his arms crossed. He is acting closed off. These guys are so confusing. I never know which side of them I will get. Not bothering to respond to Landon, I focus back on my computer. Hudson slaps the top of the desk again, "My brother was talking to you!" He raises his voice.

My heart is racing. "I know. Sorry, yes. Give it ten

minutes, then you can leave. If you leave before then, it will be suspicious."

Hudson slides his chair back and kicks his legs out, pulling out his phone from his pants pocket, joining his brother in scrolling.

Once it feels safe to do so, I look back to my computer, but I am unable to focus. My mind and body are shook, anxiety and anticipation washes through me.

"How do I give it to them? Without getting caught?" I ask, breaking the silence.

Neither of them looks up from their phones. "That's for you to figure out." Landon quietly responds.

This entire situation is stressing me out and they aren't helping. Both are acting so cold toward me. Similar to how it was before the holidays, I guess. Shaking my head of the thoughts I focus back on how the hell I am going to execute this. Each professor has their own office. If I just slide it under their door or wait until they are in there to pass it off. It should work. It has to work. Come on Banks, you can do this.

Their presence is intoxicating. Time passes quickly as I work on various other things, avoiding them. "Ok, you guys can go now."

They both stand without saying a word and head out, leaving the door open. My heart is still racing, and it feels like it could explode out of my chest.

"Banks. Sorry, Ms. Lewis." It's Coach.

I swallow almost choking from the shock of him bursting in. This is all too much.

"Coach Taylor." I smile because my brain won't function telling me what else I should do.

"Any plans for Spring Break? I know you spent the holidays alone, which is a real shame. Would you like to hang out? I guess that is what I am wondering..." Oh my word, Coach is asking me out. The man is at least twice my age, not that there's anything wrong with that. I love a good age gap novel, but no. Not him. I am not at all attracted to him.

My eyes widened, "Oh, no, Coach. No, thank you. I'm not at all attracted to you like that. If that's what you're asking?" I know my face is making a face, but I cannot control it. I am shocked. He walks around my desk and looks, squinting his eyes at me.

"The fuck you say to me, Lewis?" I'm taken aback by his tone. He is speaking to me like I am one of his players, a complete one-eighty switch in his demeanor.

"Oh, don't look at me like that. Crying won't work on me, save that shit for someone else. I wasn't asking you on a date. I felt bad for you and didn't want you to be alone if you didn't have to be." Then, it happens so fast, my skin tingles then burns, a loud crack can be heard and I go into complete shock. My mind and body freeze.

The way he's looked at me lately or the lingering touch in the locker room, which did not go unnoticed, would make me believe otherwise. He likes me, and now he is embarrassed that I rejected him.

If he only knew how I spent Christmas break. I was alone, but also very not alone, depending on the time.

I don't respond, not wanting to escalate the situation or draw further attention to my office with the door being open. Since I am also shit at confrontation, I change the subject, trying to ignore the throbbing feeling on the side of my face. "I just met with the twins, they are on track for a successful mid-term. They should be ready to go after spring break with no issues." My lips tremble with each word, but I will not let him win. I will not cry in front of him or show weakness by holding my face.

Coach Taylor rolls his eyes at me, making me feel

further belittled. This is an encounter I did not expect with him today, or ever, if I am being honest.

He turns and walks away from me. The floodgates open and my tears flow freely down my face.

Before he walks out of my office, Coach turns back around to face me. "I'm sorry, Banks. I was out of line. Your reaction, the rejection, caught me off guard and I reacted how I would if you were one of the guys on the team." Coach Taylor doesn't wait for a reply before turning back around and leaving. The audacity.

I let a deep breath out. I'm still in shock that he slapped me. He actually did it, he put his hands on me. When I stand up, my knees tremble, my hands shake, and my heart is racing as fast as my mind is. I reach the door to close it, but Hudson barges in, looking like he could rain terror down on this whole place. His eyes look almost black and his fists are clenched.

"What was that about? Did he do this to you? Did he make you cry, Banks? Why is your cheek red? Tell me." He grabs both of my shoulders, walking me backwards.

I sniffle, unable to hold it in now that attention has been brought to my current state. My lip quivers, "It's ok, Hudson. It's been a long day and I am just being sensitive."

His face hardens and he lets go of me, briskly walking out of my office. I hear him yelling, "Landon!" Ah shit.

They both walk back in seconds later.

Landon examines me, head to toe. "What's this?"

Shaking my head, I put my hands up. "It's fine. He apologized and there is nothing to worry about. It's been a long day and like I told Hudson, I am feeling over sensitive."

Hudson shakes his head, "No. I don't accept that. No one takes that tone with you. No one speaks to you like that. No one puts their fucking hands on you. Only we

213

can. Only ever us."

Coach walks back in, he must have heard the boys. "What are you two doing in here?" Hudson's face is full of rage. He is seeing red. I know that look. It's dangerous. His eyes are blackened and focused on his target, Coach Taylor.

"I heard how you spoke to her. Is that your handprint on her? Did you fucking mark her? It's one thing to treat us like shit, but not her. Never. Fucking. HER!" Hudson is shouting.

He takes a step forward. Shit.

Landon interferes, stepping in front of his brother, and in the blink of an eye, his fist connects with Coach's jaw.

I gasp, covering my mouth with my hands.

"No one makes her cry." His voice seethes with disgust.

Coach's face is bright red as he adjusts his jaw. "You're off the team. Done. OVER! Get your shit and get the fuck out of here, Landon."

Landon does something out of character and curtsies before saying, "Gladly." Then spits at Coach's feet before walking out. My eyes move to Hudson. He doesn't speak immediately, "Him and Raiden. We need him! What is wrong with you?" He questions in disbelief.

"Your brother ended his time on the team the minute he stepped up to me, and his fist connected with my face. He is done. You don't assault your coach and get away with it!"

"What about school? He needs to finish his degree." Hudson argues. I can tell when the idea has formed in his mind. With a smirk, he looks at his coach. "You know what? He isn't off the team. He isn't risking his schooling. And do you know why? Because you won't say shit about this to anyone, or I will tell them what you did to Ms. Lewis. Coming on to her. Touching her inappropriately.

Yeah, we saw that before Christmas. Making her feel uncomfortable. Yelling and slapping her when she rejected you. You will be done. OVER! You don't put your hands on her, do you fucking understand me?" He is vibrating with anger. Coach just stands there, speechless. But Hudson isn't done.

"Did I mention that we have friends in high places? We can easily make it look like you're a major drug distributor on campus. Venom, have you heard of it? Kick my brother off the team, and I will make sure you hear that name every day of your miserable fucking life. They will raid your house and office, and you'll sit in jail for the rest of your fucking life. We'd make sure you are labeled as a woman beater. You wouldn't last twenty fucking minutes in there." Hudson threatens his coach, knowing he can get away with it. "Now, I'll go let Landon know he isn't gone. You leave her alone, understand?" Hudson points at me.

Coach doesn't respond, his face is pale. He nods once and leaves the room.

I break down, my knees buckle, and my body falls on the ground. I cover my face with my hands as I kneel on the cold, cement floor rocking back and forth. I feel Hudson join me.

"Let it out. Let it all out now and then move forward. You are stronger than this, Banks. I know you are. We know you are," he whispers and moves a piece of my hair behind my ear, then moves one of my hands off my face with his, and kisses a tear falling down my cheek with his soft lips.

"You survived us. You can survive anything, Banksy."

My body shivers. He's right. I am strong.

Removing my other hand, my cheek feels like it has its own pulse, still throbbing from Coach's brutal slap. I wipe my tears away and try to compose myself. Taking deep breaths in and out help, focusing on that clears my mind.

"Good girl, Banksy. It doesn't look like it will leave a mark, but it's still a bit red. Keep breathing." He praises me. It makes me feel good and a smile forms on my face, so he knows it too.

"I am going to find Landon now. Let him know what I said to coach so he is still on the team. You do what you have to do this week, Banksy. Keep being my good girl, ok? Then text me when it's done."

Hudson leans in closer and kisses my cheek, not letting it linger. It's quick but it still sends shocks throughout my body.

"Yeah, go find Landon. Thank you, Hudson. Thank your brother for me too, please. He didn't have to do that, but he did. I appreciate that more than you will ever know." I whisper back.

"We know," is all he says before adding a wink. It melts me internally. He stands up and walks out of my office, leaving me alone.

You can fucking do this, Banks. You are stronger than this. We will get through it. I reassure myself as I walk back to my desk, drying my face with the sleeves of my sweater.

I grab my computer and decide to call it a day. We don't have a game tonight, just a practice, so I am heading home and saving fuck off to this day with a bottle of wine.

CHAPTER 30

LANDON

Exams are over. We are waiting for a message from Banks confirming she completed her part of our agreement. She has been radio silent all week. We have been keeping an eye on her from afar, not wanting to make our connection to her obvious. Last thing we need is rumors to start. They wouldn't be wrong, I did fuck her, but that's no one's fucking business.

I don't regret punching Coach. Hudson would have if I didn't. The guy is already on probation with the team. He doesn't need an assault charge and being kicked off added to his resume of accomplishments this year. So I did it. He made her fucking cry. Only Hudson and I can make her cry, and she is so pretty when she does, but not when

Coach did it.

It shocked me too. Coach can be a dick to us, but being one to her crosses the goddamn line. Anyone on the team would have done the same if they were in our shoes. She is sweet, not so innocent, Banks Lewis.

But they don't know that. They don't know her like we do. Her ticks, her breathing patterns when she sleeps, the way she crinkles her nose when she is thinking really hard on something. How her body moves under Hudson as he marks her, as I mark her. I felt instant, murderous rage hit me hard when I saw her crying. She is ours to do with as we fucking please, not for him.

After being told I was kicked off the team, I immediately went to my locker and started packing it up, that is, until Hudson walked in with the biggest shit-eating grin on his face, telling me how he'd blackmailed the bastard and I was staying. Fuck yes, let the games begin, motherfucker.

I'm in my room, starting to work on my piece that I will put over my newest scar compliments of our father. I have to wait a few months before I can ink over it, scars take fucking forever to heal, but no better time to sketch like the present.

The details of the piece I am working on are straight from my memory. I'm still debating if I will add color or keep it black and gray. Either way, it will be stunning.

Checking my phone for the eight hundredth time, still nothing from Banks. It's Saturday night, spring break is full on, and there's no faculty or students left on campus. What the fuck is the hold up here?

Pushing up from my chair, I grab my phone and keys and head out of my room, "Hudson. Let's go."

He pokes his head out of his room door, confused.

"I'm going out, bro."

"Yeah, with me. Let's move. We have a certain pet to

check in on."

Hudson smirks, the corner of his lip raising, he follows me out of the house and into the Rover, rubbing his hands together. "Banksy, our little girl has been naughty?"

I chuckle at Hud. "Yeah, she fucking has."

We listen to music the entire drive to her place. Pulling up, we can see her front room light is on. Where else would she be?

Getting out of my car we head up to her front door. I turn the knob, the odds are low it will be unlocked. She's a single female in a college town after all.

Hudson gets right in there, banging on her door with his closed fist. I'm shocked he isn't shouting and at the same time, grateful. We don't need any added attention.

I cover the peephole with my finger when I hear her approaching the door. The locks click and she opens the door slightly, leaving the chain lock on and exposing part of her face. "Really?" Is all she says, and rolls her eyes at us.

Nope, not happening. Hudson must have the same thought. It takes no effort at all once he wraps his hand around the door, forcing it open. The chain breaks off the wall and we walk in, closing the door behind us.

Her cute nose crinkles in frustration. Banks is wearing thin sleep shorts and an oversized tee and her long dark hair is up in a ponytail. Perfect for gripping.

"You fuck us again, or are you just being a complete bitch?" I ask through clenched teeth, getting right in her face.

She pushes me back, and I stumble slightly, not expecting it.

"What are you even talking about? Why are you here?"

I step toward her, closing any distance between us. "No text," is all I need to say.

Banks' face changes from frustration to confusion. "I

did, you psychopath."

Keeping eye contact with her, I shout to my brother, "Check your phone, you get anything?"

"Nah, man. Not a word from our old pal Banksy."

I raise my eyebrows at her, waiting for her excuse.

"I did. I'll show you!" She shouts at us, offended we would even question her this time. Walking around me to her couch, she grabs her phone and scrolls, then almost instantly her face drops. "I forgot to hit send. You guys, I forgot to hit send!"

"Naughty, naughty Banksy," my brother tsks.

"I did everything on Monday. From last semester and this one. I made sure no one saw me and it went down without any issues." She pleads with us as she explains.

My back is still facing her as I roll my eyes, stupid Banks. "You kept us waiting all fucking week, just to tell us you forgot to hit send? Didn't you think it was weird we didn't reply?"

"Not really. You two are hot and cold toward me. I just assumed it was a cold moment," her voice has gone all cutesy. She is sassing.

Turning around, I grab her, tossing her over my shoulder, "Get the lights Hud. She won't be back for a while."

Hudson is laughing at me as I hear him flick the switches.

"No! You cannot do this to me again. I did what you said. It's done!" Banks screams while punching my back, which has no effect on me. We head out, Hud closing and locking up behind me.

She continues her assault on me as we head to the Rover. I throw her in the back seat, then click the child locks on before closing the door. Heading to the otherside, I do the same thing. She's not going anywhere.

Getting in the car, Hudson looks back at her as we pull away and teases. "Don't try anything. You know how much we like to punish you, Banksy." Which only enrages her further. Looking in the rearview mirror, I can see her fists clenching and nostrils flare.

She did this to herself, yet again. The girl must love getting punished.

"You took away my last break, now this one. I fucking did it. I DID IT!" She shouts. I tune it out, not letting it bother me. Hudson, on the other hand, doesn't take kindly to it. "Shout at us again and I will have Hudson get the wand out. He has been dying to use it on you. We will get the wand out and you will never fucking come again in your life. Understood?"

She doesn't respond. I bet she is vibrating at this point.

And soon, she will be vibrating under and on top of us.

CHAPTER 31

HUDSON

Color me surprised. Here I was getting ready for a night out with some guys not on the team. I hadn't seen them in a while and was looking forward to a crazy night of chaos. Maybe try giving fucking another go without picturing Banks with my cum all over her tits. But this is so much fucking better.

The agent I don't have has a call set for tomorrow to discuss my possible options. I let him know I want to sign out of college, so he has been casually putting feelers out. I haven't told Landon yet. I will once I know more, like possible teams who may have interest in me. No need to get him excited yet.

The guy wants to own his own tattoo shop and do art.

He can do that from anywhere. Where I go, he goes and vice versa. That has always been our rule. Then we can raise our middle fingers up at our father and officially cut every tie left to the evil bastard.

Landon will have to keep our Banksy Boo quiet during that, or I will have to dip out to my car. Can't have my agent who is not my agent, knowing we like to kidnap our team advisor regularly.

Banks has given us the silent treatment since we snatched her. Not that it bothers us.

Looking back at her when we pull up to the house, I see her arms are crossed and she has a cute little pout on her face. "You did this to yourself—"

She interrupts me, "I have heard all of this before. But I am not going back into that fucking basement!" Banks says, seething. Her eyes are screaming murder. This is going to be fun, I chuckle at the thought.

"No, sweet Banksy, we have bigger plans than the basement this time. Don't we, brother?" My eyes remain on her, how her body reacts to every single one of my words. The chill that moved up her spine, the hitch in her breath, the slight squirm she does with her hips. I see you, Banksy.

"She has no fucking idea how bad it will be this time for her. She will be punished accordingly for the crime committed. Failure to communicate, that's a big infraction." Landon taunts.

Her eyes move between us, unsure what is to come . I stay sitting in the passenger seat, as Landon gets out and opens the back door. Wasting no time, he grabs her leg and drags her toward him. Banks tries to grab a hold of the backseat, but it's too late and he is too strong to be stopped.

Before he takes her out of the car fully, he grips her face

with his hand. "Fight me. I dare you."

Then, she does something which shocks the shit out of me, she spits at him. I mean a full on 'fuck you' hate spit directly onto his left eye. Biting my fist, I wait for his next move.

Blinking a couple times, he uses the back of his hand to wipe it away. "You like when we mark you, Banks? Because you won't like this next one." Landon promises, turning his head slightly as anger radiates off him.

She doesn't cower from it, Banksy sits up, getting directly in his face. "Sounds fun."

My dick is hard, pushing against my pants. This is so fucking hot. She is playing our games. She is matching our depravity. Or at least she's trying to, and its a fucking good effort.

In the blink of an eye, Landon has her over his shoulder again. She doesn't fight it. Instead, Banksy goes limp, like this is a completely boring experience.

I am so turned on.

Getting out of the Rover, I rush behind them as we head inside. He takes her upstairs and walks toward his room, "Get the wand."

Rushing to my room and rummaging through all my shit, I find it, along with this new pinwheel attachment I purchased. I have been itching to use this on her. I ordered it too late, it didn't arrive in time the last time Banksy was here.

This pinwheel attachment needs to be used on her pale skin. It's supposed to feel like a knife cutting the skin or intense burns when each sharp points roll across the skin, hot sparks flicker from each spike. If you don't get off from pain, then it's purely for torture.

I rush into my brother's room with it. He has her on his bed, she still isn't fighting. Which is pissing him off.

Landon grabs the ropes from when she was here last time and begins to tie her up. Banksy looks over at me and winks. She's getting off on pissing him off. Sneaky little minx.

I plug in the wand and show it to her. Based on the wide-eyed look on her face, her heart must have dropped into her stomach. Then I place the new pinwheel attachment on it, and her head begins shaking. Banksy tries to get out of the restraints, her arms pulling against them, but they are too tightly done around her tiny wrists to escape.

"Yeah, not so fucking funny anymore, is it?" Landon says as he does the final tie around her ankle. He walks up the bed, leans over and whispers. "Open." She presses her lips tightly together.

Landon grips her face, forcing her mouth to open slightly, then spits in it. "Sweetheart, you really should have behaved back in the car. But you always have to make shit worse for yourself." He tsks.

I haven't seen this side of Landon before. He only doles out immediate punishment on the ice, or when he punched Coach. He is running this and I am proud.

He slaps her cheek and turns his back to her.

"Hudson. Play with your toy, our pet." Smiling, I turn the wand on and walk toward her.

Banksy starts to fight harder against her restraints, but nothing will work. She isn't going anywhere. Her feet are my focus. Touching the pinwheel against the bottom of her foot, I begin to roll it very slowly from her heel to her arch to her toes. Her screams echo around the room. What she is feeling right now is pain. Hot, sharp, unbearable pain tingling up her body, and igniting her senses and nerves she didn't even know she had. Between the stimulation and pain, her body doesn't know how to respond. This is torture for her and so much fun for me.

Then using the same line I used to go up, I slowly move the pinwheel down.

"No. Please stop. Please, Hudson." No need to look up at her. I know tears are streaming down her face, and it brings a smile to my face.

I'm mesmerized, focused entirely on my movements.

"Should I bring Katie over, have her suck my cock while you watch instead? It wouldn't be the first time we would have an audience." I know it hurts her. If she is feeling half of what my brother and I are, she hates what I just said.

"Do it. Just fucking do it," she yells, as a tiny moan escaping from between her lips. Her body and mind are so confused. But I think it's perfect. Reacting just how I want it to.

"Landon, grab my phone. Put Katie on speaker."

He digs in my pocket as I move to the top of her foot now, the skin is thinner here with so many tiny bones. It's going to hurt like a rib tattoo would.

"Hey Hud, what's up?" Katie's voice comes over the speaker.

"I need my cock sucked. Want to come by?" My focus is on Banksy and her facial expressions. Her head shakes from side to side as I move my index finger to my lips. Hush now, Banksy.

"I'm out right now, but I can swing by later."

Thinking about it, I place the pinwheel on the top of her foot, and she struggles to work through the pain and sensations. Her mouth opens to scream, but nothing comes out, her eyes are squeezed shut as tears stream down her cheeks.

"Nah, it's fine. Another time maybe." I respond then Landon hangs up.

I move the wand from her toes to her shin, and small sparks do come off it. "Please stop. Please." Banksy pleads.

"Stop being so pathetic. Take it. Accept it. Be stronger!" I shout back at her.

Landon moves back beside her, taking his hand, he shoves it down her sleep shorts and smirks. "Soaked. You are such a liar. You fucking love this."

"Tsk, tsk, Banksy. You love this, don't you? Don't you? Answer me!"

"Yes, no. Sort of. Shit." She cries out.

Landon is finger fucking her. Her hips buck and grind against him. Using him to get herself off. I move the pinwheel further up her leg, closer to her aching pussy. More moans and screams echo throughout the room.

My fingers trace along her inner thigh for added stimulation, "Now be a good fucking girl for us, cum."

"Her pussy is dripping." Landon boasts as Banksy's body shakes in ecstasy. Her back arches as her orgasm radiates through her. The wand is still on, running havoc on her body. Her head tosses side to side, and she is panting.

As it flows through her, her body begins to calm down, relaxing against the bed. I switch the wand off, placing it off to the side. Landon brings his hand out from her shorts, his fingers glistening with her release. He holds his fingers up to me, showing me. Unable to help myself, I put them in my mouth, sucking her sweet release off each of his fingers. She is delicious. He's shocked when I lick the last finger, but doesn't show it.

Banksy looks exhausted from the overstimulation. Looking down her legs, a tiny line of a burn mark runs from her toes to her thigh. The wand. Fucking beautiful. I hope it stays, though I doubt it will. But knowing I put it there, that I marked her again, fills my chest with pride.

Landon begins undoing her restraints, her body still limp, not trying to fight him.

I kneel on the bed next to her, using my forefinger and

thumb to pinch her hard nipple. She bites her lip, turning her head toward me as her eyes trail up my body. There's no hate in her eyes like a part of me had hoped. Her eyes are soft, not angry, as they flutter before closing and she falls asleep.

Who is this girl?

CHAPTER 32

BANKS

After the adventures of last night, I passed out until morning. My body was exhausted. By the end of it, I wasn't even mad. These boys want to possess me as much as I want to possess them. They show me with pain and torture. Me submitting to it after putting up a fight, is how I show it back.

I do have some self respect, I won't give in that easily, ever.

My body aches when I roll over and my chest runs into a hard body next to me.

Hudson.

His masculine scent gives it away, even when my eyes remain closed. Wrapping my arm around him, I big spoon him. He wiggles his perfect hockey ass into the curve of my pelvis, then places his giant hand over mine, cuddling me closer. My face nuzzles between his shoulder blades, his warm skin against mine. I could stay like this forever.

Landon being here would complete it. Except he isn't here. My time in the basement heightened my sense of the guys, and helps me know if either are around.

"I can hear your mind from here, Banksy. Landon is probably downstairs, in the kitchen, thinking, since we are still in his sacred space."

My head nods against Hudson's back, his voice is deep and full of sleep.

"He isn't mad Banksy. He is processing. Trying to figure out how it's all going to work. Which is good. Let him sort his shit now. This isn't the only thing he needs to process. I still haven't told him I'm signing directly out of college. A few teams have shown interest after my 'not agent' contacted them. I just need to figure out where would be the best fit. I am basically deciding his life for him at the same time as my own. I'm not entirely sure how he is going to feel about it."

We lay in silence as I absorb it all. What are we? When they leave, I'll be alone again. They turned me into a monster with the cravings that they put inside of me. And now they are just going to leave me.

"He doesn't know?"

Hudson rolls over to face me, shaking his head, then whispers, "Just you." Before I can question him, he kisses me. Usually morning breath is an immediate ick for me, but not his. Electricity zaps on my lips the moment we connect. We use each other as a source of oxygen, breathing in deeper with each second we are connected, needing more and more. Our hips grind against each other, his cock is rock hard as it teases my aching pussy.

Fuck it.

My hands reach for his boxers and pull them down as we continue to devour each other. He doesn't stop me. We haven't fucked yet. The anticipation, the build up, has been torture. But it's what these boys do best.

His hand moves to my panties, moving the crotch piece to the side, my leg wraps over his hip for better access. Hudson wastes no time thrusting into me. A moan escapes my mouth as we continue kissing. Never breaking it.

Hudson holds my body close, fucking me like it's our last day. His hips buck against mine, he pounds into me harder and faster with each thrust. My pussy is soaked, and my clit has a mind of its own. Every time we connect she grinds against him, if even just for a moment. This feels so fucking good. He is more gentle than Landon, which surprises me.

His cock rubs against my sensitive walls as they clamp down around his shaft. I feel empty each time he pulls out, but he always comes back. Breaking our kiss, my breath is heavy and our foreheads touch. I look up at him, his eyes as heavy as mine. My heart feels like it could beat out of my chest. He grips my hips harder and whispers, "Hold on, Banksy."

Which confuses me, until he rotates us so I'm on top of him. My hands rest on his muscular chest, as his hips and cock begin their frenzy, rapidly assaulting my pussy. My back arches when he slaps my ass, the sting is immediate and it lingers, but it feels so fucking perfect as my body begins to tingle.

I've missed this. I've gone from not fucking anyone at all to craving the most depraved versions of it. This might be vanilla compared to what else we've done, but they can do their worst and it will never be enough anymore. This can never end.

Next thing I know, he is gripping my hair, pulling it down and making my head lean back. Tiny stings of pain spring up on my scalp from the hair pull. The orgasm rippling through my body gets even stronger.

"Milk my cock, Banksy. Fucking milk it," Hudson pants.

I grind down on him, and my orgasm erupts from within me. I never want this feeling to stop. This is a goddamn drug, and I'm addicted.

Hudson grunts as his cock continues to pound inside of me. Loud moans leave my mouth, without shame or embarrassment. I need him to know how great I feel. He needs to know what he does to me. I can feel ropes of his warm cum coating my insides, mixing with my own release.

My eyes roll back, and he pulls my hair harder. My body takes all the pain and turns it into pleasure for me. Every sting, every thrust into my sensitive pussy, causes me to moan louder.

I wonder what it would be like fucking both of them at the same time?

As our orgasms dissipate, our bodies slow down their assault on one another.

Hudson lets go of my hair, allowing me to look down at him. I smirk. His face is red, and his chest is moving rapidly beneath my hands, I can feel his heart beating.

"Yeah." Is all he can manage to say, and a giggle escapes me.

When I move off him, I can feel our cum dripping out of me. I wish it wouldn't. I wish there was a way to keep it inside of me longer. To feel our cum all day. And add Landon's, too.

I lay on my back, staring wide-eyed at the ceiling. Who am I? Who is this girl?

After cleaning up, we both head downstairs. Landon is nowhere to be found. Maybe he regrets it. Regrets us. Again.

I hop up on the counter wearing one of his tees, which is more like a dress on me. Hudson smirks. "Yeah, you just sit there. Let me grab the coffee." Good boy, that was exactly my plan. It's the least either of them can do after kidnapping me for a second time. I expect better service this time around.

While Hudson makes coffee, I scroll mindlessly on my phone. We both startle when the side door opens and in walks Landon, all sweaty in his running gear. He pauses, taking us in, his face passive as he clears his throat and takes his earbuds out. "You two finally fuck?"

"Yeah, bro. Is that ok?" Hudson sounds nervous. Interesting. If anyone knows Landon and his mannerisms, it's Hudson.

Landon walks up to me, prying my legs open to stand between them. He grips my jaw and slams his mouth into mine. It lasts all of a moment before he pulls back. "About fucking time."

Then walks away.

Hudson and I erupt in a fit of laughter. What the fuck was that?

"Yeah, laugh it up. It only took Hudson what, three months to fuck you? You let me fuck you after a few days locked up. Remember that, Banks." Landon yells from the top of the stairs, then slams his bedroom door. My face falls, and hurt rushes through me. Hudson notices. He walks over to me, taking the spot that Landon just vacated.

"He's confused. Doesn't know what he wants. Or he does, but doesn't understand it. Landon is processing. Don't take it personally." Hudson reassures me.

"If I took anything you two have done personally, I wouldn't still be here." I remind him. He raises his eyebrows.

"You did kind of deserve it the first time, Banksy. You were very naughty and needed to be taught a lesson. This time, it was Landon. He was on edge and not able to take it anymore. I bet his skin was itching the entire week. All because you forgot to hit send."

I shrug my shoulders in response. No point in arguing, it will only end up with me being sexually tortured. Which I don't mind, but I am a bit sore from yesterday.

We spend the rest of the day watching mindless reality show television in their media area. Landon joins us after his shower, grabbing me from Hudson's cuddle and placing me on his lap instead. Junk food and takeout bins litter the table, along with a couple of beer bottles.

It's late. The guys eventually notice my eyes struggling to stay open.

"Maybe we should get you home, hey Banks?" Landon whispers into my hair.

I shake my head. "Maybe... I can stay? Another day, maybe?" Neither of them respond. Shit. This is just another fuck to them. I squeeze my eyes shut. "It's ok, I was just kidding. I didn't mean it, guys. No need to panic."

"Look at me. Look at us, Banks," he demands.

My eyes open as my head tips up, feeling intimidated and nervous about what might come next. His beautiful blue eyes stare down at me.

"Say it with confidence this time. Tell us what you want."

Fuck, they are going to make me say it again, to embarrass myself again. I shake my head in fear, I don't need to be rejected twice in a row.

Hudson reaches out to me, wrapping his fingers around my throat as his thumb pushes my chin up. "Do what he says, Banksy." Two against one, I'm the obvious loser.

Taking a deep breath, I clear my throat and with a clear, firm voice I tell them, "I want to stay tonight. Please don't take me back home until tomorrow." I smile after the last word leaves my mouth. I'm proud of myself, even if I do get rejected, in this moment I was clear with my intention.

"See, was it that hard, Banksy? Asking for what you want?"

Hudson's hand is still wrapped around me. As I nustle into Landon, I shake my head "No it wasn't."

"Then you will stay," Landon says with finality in his tone. Hudson smirks, then winks at me. Cheeky bastard knows what he is doing to me. I squirm.

Hudson's dark hair has fallen over his forehead as I watch his eyes move up my body, his hand moves from my neck slowly down my body, over my t-shirt, with just the tips of his fingers. He moves over my breast, then he moves to my stomach until he reaches the hem of the shirt.

Landon whispers in my ear, "Arms up." Which I do, inviting Hudson to remove my top.

My shirt is pulled off, and thrown to the ground. I am completely naked, exposed, with my scars and tattoo showing. Hudson leans in, his mouth latches onto my nipple, his teeth nip me, causing me to jump in surprise. He does it again and my back arches when he takes my other nipple in between his fingers and squeezes it. I am dripping.

Landon reaches under my arms, lifting me up as he stands, then places me down back on the couch.

"On your hands and knees. Hudson, front or back?" I do as instructed, but in a state of confusion. What does he mean front or back? I don't need to wait long to understand it.

Hudson gets up and walks around to my backside, shimmying his sweats off and tossing them next to my discarded top. Landon lowers his pants next, his cock is hard, precum glistening from the tip, as he walks toward my face. Kneeling in front of me, he rubs his cock along my plump lips. I lick them, tasting him. He uses his hand to guide his cock into my mouth.

"Breathe through your nose, no amount of begging will make me stop. My cock slamming into your mouth and down your throat, choking you, is all I fucking want." I nod in understanding. Hollowing my cheeks, I begin sucking his cock. His salty precum ignites my taste buds, I need more. Looking up at him through my lashes, his eyes are hooded, and he's biting his lip.

"So fucking beautiful, Banks." He praises.

I briefly forgot that Hudson is behind me until he thrusts into my aching pussy. His hands grip my hips tightly. I love when he holds me like this, or when he wraps his hands around my neck. This isn't like this morning. There's no mercy as he relentlessly pounds into me with all that he has. I know I am going to be sore tomorrow, but I love it. I feel so full. I feel overstimulated in the best way as Landon shoves his cock further down my throat, his tip causing me to gag. Saliva runs down my chin, he grabs my hair, his cock swells, his release is coming.

"You will drink every last drop," Landon rasps.

"Fuckin' right, she will brother, or she will be punished," Hudson threatens, still pounding into me. Taking it from this angle is new, and I love it. It feels so different.

Our bodies are slapping together, and just when I think this couldn't get any better, Hudson rasps, "Next time, we are taking both holes." He spits on my backend, I feel it running down and hear him chuckle with satisfaction.

Landon works my mouth harder, his head is thrown back as his salty, warm release fills my mouth and throat. His hands grip my hair harder and his hips buck into me relentlessly. His abs flex as his orgasm continues to release into my mouth. I swallow every bit of his seed as he instructed.

My eyes water from a lack of oxygen, but I am getting off on this too. I know Hudson is about to cum. His grip on my hips is getting tighter. So is mine, on his cock. I am squeezing it, needing to feel every inch inside of me.

Landon's movements slow as his orgasm subsides. But he continues to keep his grip tight and his cock inside my mouth. My body tingles, it runs down my spine as a muffled moan leaves me.

My legs tremble, it's getting harder to keep myself in this position, my body wants to collapse.

"Cum," Hudson demands and my body responds.

We cum together. Again, he fills me for the second time today.

We ride it out, using each other to milk every last drop. As our movements slow, our panting is all that can be heard.

Finally, Landon lets go of my hair and pulls out of my mouth. I swallow, taking in everything now that his invasion has ended.

He uses his thumbs to wipe the tears under my eyes. "Such a good little girl for us, Banks. You did so good. I am so proud of you." Landon praises me, with a softness in his blue eyes.

Hudson pulls out next, "She was made for us, brother." I look up at Landon, curious about if he feels the same.

"I know."

CHAPTER 33

LANDON

It's Saturday. Time to take Banks home.
She asked to stay another night, and it turned into five.
Five days of fucking.
Her pussy is sore and probably bruised from all the poundings we have been giving her. We offered to give her a break, but she refused each time. Who are we to refuse a lady?
The three of us are in my bedroom, our homebase over the break. Hud and I haven't done a single hockey related workout except for copious amounts of cardio.
I've learned that Banks and my brother love their sleep. I'm always up before them, which isn't even early. When

we aren't fucking, we are attached at the hip.

Hudson watches game footage while Banks reads on her phone and I sketch. It's effortless. Hud and I have never shared a girl before. It never interested me. But this feels natural, right. Bringing a third person into our circle hasn't disturbed anything, it's only enhanced it.

Who fucking knew the narc locked in our basement would turn into this? That Banks would be our other person, our *only* person outside of each other.

She pissed me off with her prying. Caring about me. It took me a while to sort that shit out in my head. Hud and I are used to only having each other. Having someone else want to care at that level hasn't been something I could easily accept.

I fought this. My mind was conflicted. Not sure what to do with these feelings. If my mom was around, I could have gone to her about this. But our bastard father took that away from us. The opportunity to have a female help mold us, guide and shape us into better fucking men.

I shake my head, trying to rid my mind of those thoughts. It's irrelevant now. She is gone. Both Hudson and I know what he did to her, even if it's never been proven.

Karma is real.

I lean back in my desk chair, the table lamp is on, and my sketch pad is open with a pencil in my hand. Drawing her delicate body, tangled in my black silk sheets, her black hair hanging slightly over her face. What started as a *fuck you* over Christmas has turned into something much deeper.

At first, I was confused. When I connected with her in the basement, it wasn't something I thought would happen, it just did. I have been battling my feelings ever since.

Thinking about her, not wanting to think about her, wanting to bump into her in the hallway, and not wanting to be anywhere near her. She pried into my life, and she fucked with my brother's future.

But all that shit has fallen to the wayside now. We had a taste, saw her cry, and we became immediately protective of her. She is ours now.

No one at school can find out. She will lose her job. Hudson would lose any chance of going pro if a scandal like this hit the headlines or scout reports. This would be the one time father would actually be proud of us.

Banks shifts in bed, her slender leg wraps around the sheet, exposing her bare hip. I adjust the sketch to reflect her current state. She is stunning.

How are we going to make this work?

"Landon. Are you drawing me like one of your French girls?"

My brother is a fucking idiot.

"I'm sketching Banks." I whisper-shout at him, not wanting to wake our girl. Hud rubs his eyes and looks at his phone, it's past eleven in the morning. Getting up, he heads to the bathroom, I hear him pissing into the toilet.

"Why does he have to be so loud?" Banks groans, burying her head in my pillow.

"It's the only volume he has."

Dropping my pencil, I stand up and crawl onto the bed, pulling her close to me. She snuggles against me.

"You have to get up. We have to take you home today. Coach has us bag skating tomorrow." I whisper into her hair. She smells like me from using my shampoo and body wash. I love it.

Her fingers brush over my scars, my ink. "We haven't talked about how this is all going to work. If it's going to work?" My skin goosebumps. At the same time, Hudson comes back and hops back into bed.

"We will figure it out. This is only just the beginning. I don't know what it is exactly, but it's not something we can just stop." Hud rakes his fingers through his messy hair, his face conflicted. There aren't any right answers right now, at least not while we are still in school and she is our advisor.

"Hudson, I would never want to jeopardize your future. Or yours, Landon. And if Groveton found out about this, I'd be fired. This is a major policy violation. I'd be blacklisted until the end of time. I'd have to move and find a new career. We all have a lot at risk, just in different ways..." Banks adds. Her voice shows parts of worry and sadness.

"We are all fucking adults. What does it matter? This is bullshit. We already work the drug tests, and professors. What's one more thing?" Hudson adds.

My brother is such an idiot. "Jesus Christ. So, Banks," I close my eyes, blowing out a deep breath before continuing. "Our father is useful for one thing, he knows the people who do our random drug tests. We let the guys know once we find out, and we only use Venom because it is undetectable."

She doesn't say anything for a moment, absorbing the latest bomb of information we are trusting with her.

"Ok. So... Ok. Is there anything else?" She questions.

Hudson wastes no time. "Raiden and his crew, including Flynn and Adams, make Venom. They call themselves the Noxious Boys." Banks sits up, and her brows furrow.

"No, Adams is a recovering addict."

"Venom isn't addictive. It's the world's greatest drug, and they invented it. It's what we drugged you with at the old Grange Manor." Banks looks at Hudson.

"I don't think I should know anything else. Unless it

directly affects me. I feel like this is good enough for now."
I laugh at her, bringing her back close to me.

Banks whispers into my chest, "What have I gotten into?"

"So much fucking trouble, and you love it."

BANKS

The guys dropped me off back at home an hour ago. I went straight to the bath and loaded it with epsom salts. My kitty is sore from the pounding it's taken all week.

Soaking in the tub, I think about when it changed from a game to actual feelings and deeper emotions.

It had to have been that day when the guys found me crying with Coach. They defended me without hesitation, no questions asked. I saw them in a different light then. From vindictive and vengeful to protective and caring.

I was scared at first. Not sure if I should even trust myself after that first night during spring break. Was it only because my brain was full of lust and running on endorphins? But as the week went on, it proved to be real. The three of us fed off one another, needing more and more with each waking moment. Even with that, I think it's only natural to have your mind wander.

I haven't heard from them since we separated. Maybe I am overthinking, but maybe not. None of us know what's going on, but we are going with it. Seeing where it takes us.

I submerse myself under the water. Why am I even entertaining this? My dad would be mortified by my behavior. My chest tightens, and I bring myself back up above the water. My breathing increases rapidly.

My phone is on the bathmat next to me. I reach for it

and open our group chat the guys made before leaving.

> You both drugged and kidnapped me. How is this not fucked up?

Three dots appear immediately . . .
Hudson replies

> It's hitting you now, isn't it? You are freaking the fuck out, now that you are alone?

> **Hudson:** Perhaps?
> Breathe. Stop overthinking it. That was then, this is now. You know that.

> **Landon:** You're right. I am just freaking out
> Banksy. Just think of my cock pounding into your pussy. It'll help. It's what I am thinking about right now as I jerk off in my bedroom.

> **Hudson:** Dude. How is your dick not raw?

> **Landon:** LOL. Night guys...
> GN Banksy

> **Hudson:** Night ;)

Landon

I drop my phone to the ground, resting my head against the edge of my tub and relax. One more day until I'm back in the real world.

CHAPTER 34

HUDSON

Between classes, hockey and keeping up regular appearances at parties, it's been hard seeing Banks outside of school, but we manage. If Coach calls me in his office for some shit, I take the long way around so I can walk by her office first, sneaking in for a kiss if her door is open.

We explained the first week back after spring break that we would have to still go out so no one suspects shit. She didn't care at all, which was shocking; most chicks would be properly pissed. Not Banksy, though. Not a jealous bone in her body, apparently. We don't fuck around on her, so there isn't a need to be jealous.

She hasn't mentioned our excessive drug use at these

parties. It's not like she sees it, but she knows about it. We don't do it around her, it's not her scene. This time, we shocked her. Us giving a shit is apparently very shocking. I mean, I suppose it is, but who we were in December, is not who we are now. Completely different circumstances that we will never live down. And we can't really blame her, can we?

It's late on a Tuesday night, and there's a few of us left in the gym. The playoffs are coming, then hopefully the championship game, so Landon, Lynx, Smiley, and I are getting extra workouts in. This shit is about to get intense, the best of the best battling it out for the title of the greatest hockey team in our conference. This is our last chance to claim it, and we *will* fucking claim it. There were more guys here earlier, but they started trickling out an hour ago. I called it, and made it mandatory for the team. We need to be fucking prepared.

Landon is first to get up from his weight equipment, and, wiping his face with his white hand towel. "Heading out."

I look at Raiden and Lynx, they nod, silently acknowledging what I just asked. I get up and follow him out, taking the long way to the locker room.

Landon walks ahead of me down the hall then stops at her open door, he looks at me and grins, then opens the door. I wait outside until he comes out, holding her hand in his. She looks tired. We need to fix that.

I step forward, startling her.

"Sorry, Banksy," I chuckle and slap her ass as she moves ahead of me. She is in her signature black leggings with an oversized team tee.

"Where are you two taking me? I still have a bit of work to do." She is suspicious. I like it. Landon continues to lead the way down the hall, before stopping at Coach's office. His light is off, and the door is open.

Perfect.

Landon turns back to me and winks. It's game time.

Keeping the lights off, he leads Banksy in. I follow and close the door behind me, shutting the blinds, then rubbing my hands together with excitement.

Time for Karma.

"We shouldn't be in here," Banksy scolds.

"Banksy, punish us. We have been such bad, bad boys." I tease, my excitement radiating off me as I skip around her.

"He made you cry. He made you feel uncomfortable, and it pissed us off. A lot. Now, it's your turn to make him feel uncomfortable. He won't know for sure, but he will feel it. He'll smell it, and know that we fucked you, right here, on top of his desk. Because you are ours. He will never have you. Ever. And this will remind him of that every fucking day."

Landon stands beside Coach's desk, he taps the end while explaining our plan to Banksy. I wish I could see her face. She's either mortified or loving every second of this. I bet it is the latter.

"What if someone..."

I cut her off, holding my hand up over her mouth. "What ifs don't count. We don't deal in what ifs." She nods in acknowledgement. I whisper in her ear, "That's my good little Banksy."

She loves being praised, pride spreads across her face whenever we do. So we try to do it as often as possible, when we sneak into her place in the middle of the night or smuggle her to our place for a bit. Giving her small smiles or quick winks in the team meetings she attends.

"Keep your hand over her mouth while I devour her pussy," Landon snarks at me. The sound of her pants being pulled down comes next, then a vibration from her attempted moan follows.

He eats her, the sounds of him sucking her clit fill the room. I can feel her body move into it, she's using his face to grind on as he continues to eat her. I can hear her wet pussy, as he is fingering her now. Then the sounds stop.

"Desk. Sit on it, legs spread. Not a fucking sound leaves those lips or Hudson will punish you. It will be more than just a spanking. He will bring out the wand and not let you cum." The threat leaves Landon's lips effortlessly.

"Yeah, Banksy. I will edge the fuck out of you if I have to. Then cum all over your perfect pretty face without an ounce of guilt. Do you understand?"

Her voice is barely a whisper, but it is loud enough that I hear her say those two magical words, "I understand."

"I'm on the desk, the side facing the door," Banksy says, as she hops on the desk. Following that, I hear Landon's pants hit the ground.

Using the light from my phone, I navigate my way to the other side of Coach's desk and take a seat in his worn out chair. Turning the phone light off, I get comfortable, pulling my shorts down to expose my hard cock. Gripping it with my hand, I squeeze it hard so it feels just like Banksy's cunt. Closing my eyes, I lean my head back, listening to everything happening just in front of me.

A sharp slapping noise is followed by a muffled yelp from Banksy. Landon speaks in a harsh but barely there whisper, "Not a sound. Isn't that what you said you understood? Do we need to stop?"

"No. I'm sorry. I just wasn't expecting it. It won't happen again." She promises.

I can hear him slap her pussy and she lets out a small gasp, not expecting it. Then the assault on her pussy begins. She has to be dripping, the way slaps between their bodies connecting is all that I can hear.

Gripping my cock harder, I work my shaft quicker. Rubbing my tip, which is leaking precum, with my thumb. While I picture how Banksy must be looking right now, just inches from me, spread open for my brother. Her head thrown back, and her back arched, with her short legs wrapped around his waist, taking every inch of him inside of her. Gripping it with everything she has, chasing the feeling she most desires.

I hope she makes a mess all over this bastard's desk, so he knows what happened here tonight. All of these perfect thoughts are enough to get me off.

My cock swells, and my movements become more rapid with need, chasing my own release. I spread my legs wider as my balls tighten, and cum shoots out of my tip. I can feel the warm release on my fingers and I continue to work myself.

Landon lets a deep grunt out, the slapping noise becomes quicker. By now Banksy must be trembling from him cuming inside her. She fucking loves when we cum inside her, it's her way of claiming ownership without people knowing, except for her and us. What a fucking woman.

My cock begins to soften as my orgasm ends. I release it and let it fall between my legs, hoping some of the excess drips onto his chair. I grin, thinking about Coach seeing our treats left behind.

"Good little girl, Banks." Landon rasps.

"Thank you," she responds sweetly through her panting. I hear movement in front of me, they must be putting their pants back on. I stand and do the same, feeling the edge of the desk to navigate myself around to the front.

My shoulder grazes hers, and I wrap my arm around

her, bringing her close to me. "You did so good, Banksy. I came from just hearing you. It was fucking perfect."

She nestles closer to me, wrapping both her arms around my torso. "Thank you, Hudson."

I kiss the top of her head when the door opens, Landon is standing in the light and I nod at him. Letting go of Banksy, we walk toward the hall, and Landon flips the blinds open again.

As we wait for him, Raiden and Adams walk by with Smiley tailing them, they give us a quick wink. Smiley is distracted by something on his phone and doesn't even look up, "Hey, Ms. Lewis. Looking fresh." Then continues his walk to the dressing room to shower and change.

Banks looks like she wants to crawl in a hole and hide.

"Banksy, those two know. We talked to them earlier, asking them to give us fifteen minutes before leaving the weight room. And, well, Smiley was just flirting with you. Like most of the guys already do." Her face is still mortified, not taking anything I have said as comforting.

"Banks. It's fine. They won't say anything. They will watch out for you. If they hear any rumblings of anyone catching on to us, they will let us know. It's ok. We got you." She nods.

"No. It's fine. It's all fine. I mean worse case, I get fired and labeled a predator of college boys. Right?" We both burst out laughing. She is the last person who would ever be considered a fucking predator.

"Don't laugh at me. This is very possible." She sighs, crossing her arms over her chest.

Landon grabs her shoulders, rubbing them and forcing her to start walking back to her office. Before they walk past me, I remind her, "We have always been the predators, and you, are our fucking prey. Remember that."

"You're not wrong. You guys kidnapped me—twice."

"Exactly." Landon responds.

We head into her office. I don't feel bad about stealing her away for a bit, it's too late in the evening, she shouldn't be working anymore. Turning around, I can see she is thinking, it's all over her post-fucked face. Her eyes go between Landon and I a couple of times, she bites her lip and scrunches her face.

We wait, watching her in return.

"You guys are the first I've had sex with in a while..." she confesses. Which kind of surprises me. It's not like she's ugly.

"I just needed you to know that. That night in the basement, it had been over a year, maybe two. I don't sleep around. And I have an IUD so don't worry. No babies. I don't think we have ever used a condom." Banks spits out in rapid fire. Fuck, the thought to even check if she was on birth control never crossed my mind. Which is completely fucked. We don't know her, we don't need children, but this helps put our mind at ease, I suppose.

"Good. Nobody else except for us will be anywhere near that pussy, got it?" Landon barks. She has changed him from a guy who didn't give a fuck about pussy to a possessive pussy freak. I still love fucking and jerking off but only to her. I tried other chicks sucking my dick after the basement, but only thinking of Banks being covered in my cum would get me off.

"Pack up and head home. We will sneak over and bring food, don't clean up. I like when you have us inside of you. And you do too." I instruct, following it with a kiss to her forehead. She smiles, proudly. Fucking right.

As I head out, Landon walks up to her, kissing her briefly and then follows me out.

"You two are so bossy!" Banksy shouts out of her office.

"And you like it, remember that!" I yell back behind

me.

"Bro, we need to talk," Landon mumbles, followed by a sigh. Yeah, I know.

We finished eating at Banksy's place and watched a movie. Landon is driving us back home when I decide to drop the bomb.

"So. I have a guy putting out feelers to pro teams, here, in the states to sign right out of college. A few have responded with interest."

He doesn't respond. His fingers tap against the steering wheel.

"Where are we headed?" His response surprises me. I thought he would be pissed. I don't know why, but I did. Making such a massive decision without him, I suppose.

"A couple on the west and one on the east are confirmed." Well, sort of, unofficially.

"It's ok. Let me know when you decide or whatever. I can take my art anywhere. You are the one more limited."

"You have no idea how relieved I am to hear this, bro. I was so nervous to talk to you about it, so I talked to Banks and she helped. I didn't want you thinking I was taking the easy way out. But really, it's a sure thing way out. It secures our future."

He looks at me, an arch in his brow, before looking back at the road. "Banks knows?"

Fuck me.

"Yeah, she was easy to talk to. I just let all my thoughts out, and she listened. I felt heard. Father never fucking made either of us feel that way. It was nice…" I explain, he is pissed that I confided in her before him.

"I get it. It's fine. Sometimes it's easy to talk to someone on the outside, get their perspective and shit. I'm not mad. I'm shocked. Really fucking shocked. But not mad. I know you are doing what's best. Go with your gut. Then let me know where the fuck we are headed to." I nod, absorbing all of this.

He has really fucking changed. So have I. Pouring my thoughts out to a chick. But she isn't just a chick. She is Banksy. Our Banksy.

CHAPTER 35

BANKS

My stomach has been nauseous all day. The guys powered through the playoffs, undefeated. Some games were insanely close, and I swear the last one I had my eyes closed more than open every time those fuckers were in our zone.

At one point, I was up out of my seat yelling. I'm sure the people around me thought I was nuts, but I am just passionate about our team. And my guys.

I call them that in my head. We haven't officially had any sort of talk about us, but there aren't any other people we are seeing. And this is so easy. Sure, we get annoyed at times, but it's water under the bridge by the end of the day. This year has been a rollercoaster.

Being nervous about starting this job and finding my footing, and then Christmas break, which nearly broke me as a person then turned me into who I am now, then everything that followed. This was not on my bingo card.

I am in my same spot that I sit in at each home game. My hair is loose, hanging over my shoulders. Even though it's spring, the rink is cold. I am in my trainers, black leggings, and my oversized team hoodie. I sent the guys a good luck text beforehand, and they sent a heart emoji in response.

But they are in the zone. They have rituals and nasty facial hair growing out of control. It's all in the name of hockey, so I support it, even if I prefer them without.

Coach has kept his distance, talking to me about work things only. I'm sure he noticed we fucked on his desk. Hudson told us he left a treat on his chair, so how could he not?

The team intro song comes on, and I feel like my heart could beat out of my chest. I have no idea how they stay so calm about it.

Most of the team's families have shown up, with the exception of their father. Which shocked me, he would love all the attention he would get from being their dad.

Apparently, his business needed him overseas, so that took priority. Which sucks for them, but I don't mind. Fuck him. It makes me sad that their childhood wasn't like mine. I wouldn't be here without my dad, he is my biggest inspiration.

Focusing back on the ice, the guys come out from their tunnel. Over the loudspeaker, they are introduced and the entire place stands to cheer them on. I get out of my seat, clapping and joining in with the screams.

Then, Baylor U hits the ice, and the arena immediately turns into boos and heckling for the opposing team. This has to be so hard. But also super motivating for them. But our guys have home ice advantage. We got this. They got this.

Once the crowd has calmed down, the first line on both teams take the ice and a local singer takes her place on the carpet laid out for her on the ice as she begins to sing the national anthem.

It's electric in here. We can't even hear her over the speakers. The crowd has taken over completely. It gives me chills. This is what sports does—makes people feel like they are a part of something.

Once the anthem is over, we all take our seats, the refs hit the ice and it's time for the first faceoff of the game. Hudson is at center, ready to take it. The puck drops in slow motion, rotating slowly as it falls to the ice, the players never take their eyes off it. Number one rule, head up, eye on the puck. And they are doing exactly that.

We win the faceoff, and he passes it to Lynx, who takes off instantly with it. The rest of his line skates around Baylor, in an effort to meet Lynx at the net.

Before they can, Smitty is checked hard into the boards. We all wince. He is a big guy, so it sounds worse than it is. He doesn't miss a beat, elbowing the dickface who did it and joining the rest of his line.

Lynx has the puck, looking for someone open not wanting to risk losing it. He passes it backwards to Raiden, who passes it to Hudson. Baylor tries to stop him, but he passes the puck through a guy's legs, meeting it on the other side and taking a shot. It's stopped by the goalie. That motherfucker.

A whistle blows and the play stops. My nails are going to be bitten off by the end of this.

The first period comes and goes. Remaining scoreless for both teams. Every time we are in each other's zones, the crowd is at the edge of their seats. All this stress cannot be good for our hearts.

The other team is good. Like really good. Fuck. But we are better. Without a doubt. I have seen these guys in practice. The team work, the chemistry and the skill. We have it all. We are a goddamn triple threat.

A whistle blowing catches my attention, Raiden has a guy by the collar of his jersey. We cannot afford to take a penalty, this game is too important.

Standing up, I shout, "Don't you do it!" My vision is laser focused and I honestly think he hears me because he raises his hands and skates backwards away from the other guy. I sit down, but it's too late. Raiden gets a two-minute penalty for roughing. Motherfucker.

Special teams are now on the ice, and it's four on five. We are a guy down and the puck is still in our zone at the faceoff. The other team is skating circles around us. They win the faceoff, and now they are trying to tire my guys out. This is not ok.

I go to stand again, but a soft hand touches mine. I turn my head to find a kind eyed older lady looking at me. "Sweetie, they will throw you out if you do it too often. Space it out, perhaps?"

She has a point. I thank her and sit back in my seat. My legs bounce uncontrollably. The other team takes a couple shots on our net, without success.

The puck bounces off Barlowe's pads and Hudson takes possession. My eyes light up with excitement. Hudson is cruising down the ice. Other than the goalie, no one is there protecting Baylor's zone.

"Go Hudson, fucking go!" I shout amongst the loud cheers surrounding me. Come on, Hudson. You got this baby. Please.

The same lady holds my hand, we both squeeze at the

same time Hudson takes the shot. My heart drops and I am pretty sure I stop breathing.

We stand up to get a better view, the goalie sticks his leg out further to the left in an effort to block the shot. It doesn't work. The puck flies right though his five hole and we fucking score.

We join in cheering and celebrating. I even hug my new friend. Tears of happiness and pride fill my eyes. He did it.

The team joins him in celebration. Embracing Hudson at the other end, rubbing his helmet and congratulating him. As he skates to the bench, the loud speakers vibrate as the goal is announced. Cheers erupt in the rink again. I can see a smile on Hudson's face through his face shield. His eyes are on me and he gives a slight nod.

I smile back, wiping a tear. He winks and I know he is laughing at me for my over-the-top emotions. But this is a big deal.

Sitting down, I let go of my new friend's hand. "You keep him. He looked for you after he scored the biggest goal of his life. You keep him. And make sure he knows how to keep you," she tells me.

"Thank you." I can't say much more than that, not wanting to draw anymore attention to this.

The score remains one to nothing as the second period wraps up and we head into the third.

The other team has been in our zone way too many times and for way too fucking long for my liking this period. I'm about ready to go out there myself and tell them to leave us alone.

I know my nostrils are flaring and I look like a crazed person, but any fucks I had about that are long gone.

Landon and Raiden have been on the ice for too long, there's been a line change already, but they can't go. Baylor is causing too much havoc around our goalie for them to switch off.

They are tired, their legs aren't moving as fast. They need a break.

Then out of nowhere, because I wasn't paying attention to the other team, Landon slides his body across the ice in front of Barlowe. He's blocking the shot.

He is using his body to block the freaking shot.

The puck is flying at a speed I can't even imagine. It connects directly with his face shield on his helmet. It's made of metal wiring and a clear half face visor, but it was not made to block shots like this.

His head jerks back, and the puck slides away. Landon immediately grabs onto his helmet, his knees curling into him. The crowd gasps, then it goes completely silent as we all watch him. Please get up. Please be ok. His loud yell echoes through the arena.

No. He's hurt. But how bad?

The nice old lady next to me holds my hand again, "He will be ok, dear. If he is hurt, you need to be strong for him. He will need it."

I look at her quickly in disbelief, "How?"

"I am old, not blind." She winks at me.

Raiden and Smiley help Landon get up. His arms go over their shoulders and they skate him off the ice and help him walk down the tunnel.

Fuck.

As much I want to be there for him, the trainers wouldn't let me near him while examining him. Plus, Hudson is still out here.

Dammit.

Tears well in my eyes. I have to be strong. I'll see him after the game, he will be fine. There's only a couple of minutes left. It's going to be fine.

The refs take back control and drop the puck in our zone for another heart wrenching faceoff. I don't know how many more I can handle in our zone.

The third line is out there, doing a great job of keeping the other team from getting any shots on net.

The clock is counting down very slowly. Is this thing working properly?

The puck is in Baylor's zone, finally, both coaches call for a line change. First lines are back out, with the exception of Landon. A guy from the second line joins Raiden on defense.

The pressure is on.

Lynx goes full force toward the puck, blocking the guy with it in the corner. Their sticks battling for possession.

Lynx gets it and shoots it out, Hudson gets it, but is immediately attacked by two of Baylor's guys.

He shoots it back to Raiden, who doesn't keep it long, passing it to Lynx.

Lynx skates around the net, trying for a wraparound. The goalie stops it, and the whistle blows, bringing us into another faceoff.

Lynx takes it.

What are they up to? We have less than a minute left. We are ahead one nothing, why do we need to try shit?

Baylor wins the face off. See? This was stupid.

They surround Baylor's guys, not letting them get out of their zone. Sticks are swiping left to right on the ice. Which is clearly aggravating Baylor. Smitty skates forward, trying to challenge the guy with the puck, trying to force him into doing something stupid.

Maybe this wasn't a bad idea.

My friend grabs my hand again. "They did it, sweetie." Before I can scold her for jumping the gun, the buzzer sounds. I hug her while bouncing up and down.

We won!

Tears run down my face when I let go of her and face the rink. The rest of the team invades the ice, the coaching and training staff follow. Then, from the tunnel, Landon steps out on the ice, still in full gear, and the crowd gets louder cheering that he is ok.

The team celebrates with each other, then forms a line to congratulate Baylor with handshakes. The ice gets set up for the trophy ceremony while that happens.

Baylor leaves the ice and some powerful hockey guy says a speech, which I truly don't care about. Just give them the trophy!

A few more minutes pass before the speech ends and Hudson skates up, accepting the trophy on behalf of the team and the school. I snap a few photos as he lifts it up, kissing it, then skates back to the team to continue celebrating with them.

I snap a couple more pictures when Landon holds it, then I sneak out of the stands. I want to be able to congratulate them in person outside of the locker room.

It's been over an hour, but some guys start to make their way out of the locker area. I decided to wait outside the double doors like a true groupie fan instead of using my staff access.

The doors swing open, Hudson bursts out of the locker room buzzing. I've never seen him so happy.

Flynn, who is a counselor at Groveton has also been out here waiting with me for his guys, moves his body next to me so his back facing me. It's odd, but I don't question it.

Hudson rushes me, grabbing my face and kisses me. I don't fight it, he deserves this. He is a champion. He pulls back slightly, still smiling, and places his forehead against mine. "Banksy, we did it." His eyes water and I love that.

"I am so proud of you, baby." I whisper against his mouth. He looks deep into my eyes and then confesses, "I love you, Banksy."

My eyes water alongside his for the hundredth time tonight.

"I love you too." I respond without hesitation.

"How do you like San Jose?"

"I don't know? I have never been." I say, confused, still overcome with emotion.

"Get packing, Banksy. We are going to play with some sharks." He winks, kissing me once more before stepping back. I am speechless. What does this mean?

Before I can question him, Landon takes his spot, wearing his sunglasses. Poor boy.

"I'll be wearing sunglasses inside for a while. No tv, minimal phone time, and loads of headaches and concussion testing. They don't know how long it will last, but I don't have any regrets. They also said no strenuous activities either, so you will have to ride my cock like a good little girl." I slap his tee shirt clad chest, but instantly feel bad.

He notices and laughs at me. At the same time, I see the place where his scar used to be is covered with a new tattoo. A green eye. I look at it, puzzled. Whose eye does he have on him? He doesn't have any colored ink on him, so this is all very odd.

Flynn is still blocking the view in the hallway for us when Landon leans forward. "It's yours."

My hands fly over my mouth, and I step forward,

closing the gap between us as I take it in. I am speechless. It's stunning. It's my eye.

"I love you, Banks."

My eyes look up at him. He moves my hands away from my face and kisses me softly. As our lips separate, I whisper back, "I love you, Landon."

"I wish you could come celebrate with us, Banksy." Hudson chimes back in. It's not worth the risk.

"I know. Me too. It's ok. You guys go have fun. You deserve it! Maybe Flynn and I will hang out?" I joke.

He turns around and immediately squashes that idea. "No."

The three of us laugh at his response.

"I won't be out long anyway. My nurse should come by later to help me though. What do you think?" Landon winks. I roll my eyes, but obviously will swing by once he gets home.

Then I remember Hudson mentioning San Jose. "Hudson, what do you mean San Jose?" He grabs my head and kisses me again, "If anyone can figure this out, it's you, Ms. Lewis."

CHAPTER 36

LANDON

The conference championship we won was at the end of March. We went to the Frozen Four in April, but sadly lost. But it was an honor to even be there. I didn't play, concussion and all, but I still went and supported. Banks went too, watching every game. She is a part of the team and I would like to see anyone say otherwise.

We haven't brought up San Jose again, it's more fun this way. She seriously doesn't get it. Or if she does, she isn't the type to assume if we don't straight out ask her. Hudson verbally agreed to sign with San Jose following graduation, which is today. Then we'll have a couple months to settle into the city before training camp starts for him. And Banks is sure as fuck coming.

Over the loudspeaker, I can hear them call for Hudson Cooper. He is in his cap and gown next to me as he stands and walks across the stage, taking his degree. Next they call me, and I follow suit.

Banks is in the crowd cheering us on. Father didn't bother coming, he knew it was pointless. All our ties are officially severed the moment the ink hits that pro contract. Hudson did it, he got us fucking out. I will never know how to thank him properly for this. But when I figure it out, I will.

Hud is there waiting for me when I walk off stage with my degree. Banks is next to him in a black crop tee, and a high-waisted black skirt that has a slit in the front, the hem is slightly below her knee and she is in her classic converse shoes. Her hair is curled and in a high pony, light make-up with the biggest fucking smile on her face.

I grab her head and push our lips against one another. I devour her, wrapping my other arm around her waist, bringing her closer to me. We kiss a moment longer before she pulls back. "What are you doing?" Banks scolds me.

I wink at her as Hudson grabs her, doing the same thing. Looking away from them briefly, I notice we have a group of eyes on us. Moving my focus back to my brother and our girl, Hudson pulls back and says, "You are coming to San Jose with us, Banksy. Fuck 'em."

He can't, but I can and will.

I drop my paper to the ground and raise both my middle fingers high, no one can stop us now. We have officially claimed her, and she has claimed us.

"Leave my Papa alone! Right, Mama?" The tiny voice shouts, sitting next to me. Smiling, I look at him, decked out in San Jose gear. "That's right, baby. You tell them, leave your Papa alone! Right, Daddy?"

"That's right, or we will have to send them into a time out, wouldn't we buddy?" Landon leans over, encouraging his crazy.

Our four-year-old son, Pax, sits between us at a home game, acting as crazed as his mother when anyone gets near Hudson and the puck.

We got pregnant pretty quick after moving to San Jose. Hudson signed with San Jose the afternoon after graduation, also hired his 'not an agent', as his actual agent just before that.

The guys wanted me barefoot and pregnant in our beautiful home immediately. Being older than them by ten years and my biological clock ticking, I couldn't disagree. I found a really great doctor here, and we got my IUD out. Once my cycles became more regular, we started trying. With a lot of practicing done too.

A couple months later, I was taking tests, and one came out positive. I took four more to be sure, which were all very positive.

After graduation, Landon and Hudson rushed me to my office in the rink, helped me clean it out and when we were in the Rover, I sent my resignation email. Later that night, I went to a couple of graduation parties with them. No longer having to hide our relationship. When the team noticed, they were so excited. It reassured me that they were making the right decision. I couldn't live without them.

Pax was an easy pregnancy and birth. Terrible baby. He hated sleep. He had to have taken after the guys, because never once did my dad mention me being a terrible baby. But we managed. Thankfully, it was Hudson's off season, so he could help out more. During the season we don't like adding extra stuff on him. Landon and I run the house during that time.

Speaking of, Landon opened his own tattoo shop a couple miles from the house. It's a perfect location, a lot of foot traffic and it doesn't hurt being Hudson Cooper's brother.

He called it Muse Ink. Apparently after me, which was such a sweet surprise and completely unexpected. The first person he inked in the shop was me. Over the grafting scar. It hurt more than I thought it would, but it turned out perfect. I got Pax and Paisley's names there in a beautiful fine line script. It symbolizes how I met and fell in love with their fathers and the beautiful family we have created after all the evil. If they ever ask, naturally we would lie, as parents do, about certain things.

Paisley is just over two and is at home with our part-time nanny. She's still too young to come to a game with us. Pax doesn't normally, but it was an early game, so we didn't see the harm in it. We don't know who fathered who, but I have my own thoughts, which I keep to myself.

The goal buzzer sounds, followed by the goal song. "Yeah! Papa!" Pax is on his feet, bouncing up and down, so excited to see his dad score. Landon grabs Pax and lifts him on his shoulders, so he can see his papa better, while we celebrate the goal.

Hudson looks over at us. We sit here each home game, instead of the wives suite, he points directly at Pax, then waves. Our little boy is so excited that I am convinced he is going to jump off Landon, trying to get to him. Hudson winks at me, before rejoining his team and the game.

I fucking love that man. Landon moves next to me, as he puts Pax back down, I look up and he kisses me. "Love you, Mama," he whispers against my lips, desire filling his eyes. We are going to have fun after the babies go to sleep tonight.

I often wake up in disbelief that this is our life. The team has been so supportive and accepting of our dynamic, never questioning it. Hudson signed a two-year contract initially, then resigned for five, we still have two years left and I hope we stay. We have placed our family's roots down here. We love our community. And the team is like our family now.

The final buzzer sounds, the game is over.

Despite Hudson scoring, the team still lost. Which is ok. We are already in contention for the playoffs. This loss won't hurt that.

"Alright little dude, let's go." Landon scoops Pax up. He is so fucking handsome with our son in his arms.

"If you are a good little girl, I will fill your pussy up with another one," he looks back at me and whispers. This man knows. Well played. I smile in response.

We wait for Hudson in the family waiting area. Pax races around with some of the other kids, and Landon has me in his arms. This will never get old. I can't wait until we can bring Paisley to a game.

The doors open, and Pax spots him first, shrieking, "Papa!" I look over, Hudson is already bent down with his arms out ready to catch our crazed demon child.

Once he scoops Pax up, he walks over to Landon and I, he notices my smile.

"Landon promised he would put a baby in me later tonight," I whisper into Hudson's ear so no one can hear us.

He chuckles. "We would be even numbered."

That's his way of agreeing.

I step back, releasing my hug with Landon. "Well, what are we waiting for? We have babies to put to bed and babies to make!"

My vision is gone. Darkness with stars is all I see. A strong hand is wrapped around my throat. Hudson is choking me, as I lay naked on our California king bed.

My body tingles. My lungs beg for air as they contract under my ribs. Any moment now I will pass out from lack of oxygen, but I fucking love how rough they are with me. I feel his cock working my aching pussy. My legs tremble around his hips and I try to gasp for air one more time. But nothing comes from my lungs.

"Fucking take it, Banksy," he rasps in my ear, and it sounds like it's coming from far away. Electricity flows through me as my orgasm hits. He can feel my pussy milking his cock, that's the signal.

He lets go just before I fade.

My eyes open, and I gasp as my orgasm feels even more intense. I can feel it from the tips of my fingers all the way to my toes, which are flared out.

Tears run down my face. I love their beautiful torture.

"Mine. Ours. We fucking own you," Landon speaks from beside us. I look over, his chest is still heaving as he catches his breath. Before Hudson took over, Landon was in my ass. I can still feel his cum leaking out of me as more fills me.

Hudson pounds into me once, his body flexes, it's bruised from the game. My hand reaches out to touch him, as he empties himself. It's my favorite feeling, being filled by them. Leaking them. As Hudson pulls out, I am still panting. He gathers Landon's release from my other hole, then shoves it into my pussy, to mix alongside his.

Then he brings his fingers to my mouth. He doesn't need to speak, I know. Opening my mouth, he puts his fingers inside and I lap them with my tongue. Tasting them both. My taste buds explode with desire. I fucking love these men.

Landon rolls over and grabs my face. "Suck them." I do. A pinch on my nipple causes my back to arch. I love their pain.

Hudson removed his fingers, and a pop sound follows.

As Landon moves closer, his lips touch mine, and I open my mouth allowing his tongue in. He likes tasting afterwards and I don't blame him, it's delicious. Hudson leans forward and licks my face from chin to forehead. Claiming me.

Using my hands. I grip them both. They get hard again, instantly.

I can feel the cold metal lining Landon's cock, he's gotten a Jacob's ladder. It feels fucking phenomenal no matter which hole he invades. My pussy is already dripping, anticipating more.

Time for round two.

ACKNOWLEDGMENTS

I mentioned on a TT live, that when I start writing a book the show I have on is the show that will be played until it is done. The lucky show for Lessons was, The Fall of the House of Usher. The crazy thing is I could watch it another hundred times and still love it.

This book...not in a million years did I picture the path that lead me to these characters. This book may not have been here if it wasn't for S.J. Ransom sliding into my DMs early last year and asking if I wanted to join in on the Groveton Shared World adventure. I was absolutely floored, she wanted me? Someone who had put out one free novella and I think Shadows had just been released. After being asked, it took me all of an hour to come up with my story line, which is Lessons from the Depraved and accept her offer. I am super grateful for you, S.J. thank you for including me in this journey.

Because of her, we have the twins and Banksy!

Thank you to my Alpha and Beta Queens! To my ARC and ST Queens and, you the Queen Readers!! I am not here without you. So, thank you for allowing me to be in this amazing community, writing my wild books.

Mr. Kincaid - he took one for the team. I asked him to proof my hockey bits, to make sure they were accurate for college hockey. He came in clutch and ended up reading it all. He didn't have too, but I think we may have flipped him to the dark side. He also learnt a new cool kid term, snatched. He was so confused when he saw it, it was adorbs.

Lori - thank you for joining the chaos! I am insanely excited for the plans we have in the coming years. That's right, years! Thank you for also proofing Lessons after the hubs did his bit. I appreciate you!

K.L my sweet sweet K.L. We did a mini crossover!! Can you believe it? And you learnt hockey in the process. Making the six tab 'KL Learns Hockey" spreadsheet was the best day ever. I absolutely adore you, love you and I am forever keeping you as my bestie.

Haaannnaahhh. My graphics warrior designer and most importantly, my friend. Thank you for being with me on this ride! I appreciate everything you do.

Amy/Bookswithag, my Lessons head cheerleader! I hope you enjoyed the book. Do you love the designated cheer for the team? Check hard, play hard, fuck hard!

That's it. That's all. Until the next one, Queens
xx Kins

REAM QUEENS

Lori Rivera
BookedupAF
Kayla
Trash Taco
Darkntwistedk
HannahReads
Arriana
Hbrock1103
Ashley
Bookswithag
Marima12502
Katelinreads
Nerdygurlreads
Kairjaycreads
Shortandsmutty
Amy - Martha Moo Moo

ABOUT THE AUTHOR

Kinsley is a Canadian, Dark Romance Author who dabbles in both Taboo and Forbidden. When she isn't plotting her next twisted book or watching true crime docs with her cats, you can find her working for the man. Reading. Or drinking wine... vodka... beer... while causing chaos with friends, let's not limit ourselves now. Make sure you follow Kins on her socials and sign up for her newsletter to see what is coming next!

authorkinsleykincaid.com

MORE FROM
THE AUTHOR

Forbidden
Let's Play - Freebie
Within the Shadows
Lessons from the Depraved
Haunted by the Devil

Taboo
Wrecked
Sutton Asylum
Dark Temptation: Part One
Ghost Dick; A Port Canyon Chronicle
Dark Temptation: Part Two
Sick Obsession - Coming 2024
F*ck Me, Daddy; A Port Canyon Chronicle - TBD

Made in the USA
Columbia, SC
26 June 2024